THE TETRAD PROPHECY

Credits & Copyright

To my loving and supportive family, Jio, Nathaniel, and Joey; I love you to infinity and beyond.

Here I go!

Table of Contents

LEXICON

Primordial God(s)
"Two – Lord" "Lord of the Duality"
Ometechuhitli (oh-mhe-te-koot-lee)
Omecilhuatl (oh-may-SEE-wah-tl)

Creator Gods
Huizilopochtli (wee-tsee-loh-poch-tlee)
Quetzlacoatl (ket-zahl-KO-wattl)
Tezcatlipoca (tez-cat-lip-oka)
Xipe Totec (zip-tou-tech)

Lord of the Night
Mictlantecutli (meekt-lahn-te-koot-lee)

Other Dieties
Nanahuatzin (nana-who-at-zin)
Tecuciztecatl (te-cu-sis-te-katl)
Mictecacihuatl (meek-teka-see-wahdl)
Coyolxauhuqui (koy-ol-shauw-kee)

Other
Tenochtitlan (the-NOTCH-tit-lahn)
Ocēlōtl (o-se-lo-tl)

CHAPTER ONE

Is this a foreshadowing of my impending death? I feel as if I'm being torn apart by an internal struggle. I have a white-hot fire inside me and yet it's not scorching me. Why is that?

Those thoughts ran through my mind as I sensed a presence nearby. Surveying my surroundings, I could see a dusting of snow over the ruins of an ancient city. The tumbled down, and decaying landscape wasn't immediately recognizable to me, and yet something about the place tugged at the edges of my memory. The fallen stone walls created a labyrinth, and upon closer examination, it was clear to me that the structures were not of my time.

Alerted by a faint vibration in the ground, I had the

sensation of not being alone as the hair on the back of my neck bristled. Spotting a faint trail, I darted along it, eager to put some distance between me and whatever had triggered my finely tuned senses. As I scanned the trail ahead, I couldn't help wondering if there were better options. *Would I be more visible on the trail? More of a target?* On impulse, I veered into the maze of tumbled walls I'd noticed earlier, trying desperately to control my breathing.

The sound of footsteps thudding on the ground behind me grew louder. My pursuers made no effort to conceal their presence.

The sensation of an internal flame returned as I fought to comprehend. Flashes of radiant energy pulsed through my body causing an awakening within the very core of my being.

The footsteps grew nearer. I felt trapped, realizing I had nowhere else to go to avoid detection. Perhaps in more glorious times, the stone walls may have offered better protection. In their crumbled condition, they were of no use at all. Mustering all my courage, I stepped out into the open.

My heart raced as I became overwhelmed with fear, facing the unknown. Panting for air, dizzy with desperation, I stood trembling.

"Please! Do not be afraid." It was a masculine voice, even though I couldn't see the mouth move.

As he drew nearer, I was able to get a better view. I realized it was a man wearing a large ceremonial headpiece. A gleaming gold eagle's head trimmed with colorful feathers.

"Who are you?" I demanded, "Don't come any closer." Scanning the area, I discovered the man was not alone. He was flanked by many similarly outfitted natives. Their headpieces were not as intricate and did not cover their faces. In place of masks, they wore face paint in a variety of designs, which I concluded must have been meant to indicate their status within the group. *Where in the world am I?*

"We are the Cuachicqueh, your warriors of the highest realm; The Shorn Ones. We are here to protect you. My name is Tadeo, the Tlacateccatl, which means General," he said, as he came to a halt directly in front of me. Breathing in his musky scent, I could feel the warmth of his body on my exposed skin. *What did he mean, my warriors?*

He removed his mask as he spoke, revealing a smudged layer of red and blue face paint similar to the others. He appeared to be a young man, perhaps close to my own age, seventeen. His features were hard and chiseled.

I was about to question him when he interrupted me.

"I don't have time to explain everything to you at this moment, but you need to follow me. Something is out there and on the move. My warriors and I need to get you to safety." He paused, looking me straight in the eyes. "I believe you've made a connection with your element, am I correct?"

"You must have mistaken me for someone else. I

don't know what you're talking about. I cannot accompany you or…" I was interrupted by a rumbling sound in the distance. It grew louder by the second but didn't seem to be coming from the sky.

"What is that?" I asked. My voice remained calm, seemingly unmoved, but my stomach seemed ready to leap out of my body.

"That is Mictecacihuatl, the goddess of the underworld and Coyolxauhuqui, the goddess of the moon. Hurry, we must leave NOW."

Driven by instinct and fear of the unknown, I followed Tadeo, as his warriors flanked us from behind.

We made haste, first along the dusty trail I'd contemplated earlier, then we moved stealthily into the woods to the left of the trail. I realized as we passed the ruined buildings, that what I thought was snow earlier, was actually ash.

I kept close to Tadeo, avoiding low-hanging branches and the thick undergrowth of the unfamiliar area. I was surprised at how silently we were proceeding.

"Where are we going?" I inquired as I ran harder to keep up with him.

"To the city. The sacred grounds of the temples will protect us from these demons, as they cannot follow us there." His words were smooth, unfazed even by the effort of running.

I felt like I'd broken through a chain of linked arms during a game of Red Rover, as we slowed down;

except there wasn't any barrier, at least not to the naked eye.

When we finally stopped, I was gasping for air, completely drained of energy. As I dropped to the ground panting, Tadeo looked down at me. The inner flame I'd experienced earlier seemed to have diminished somewhat.

"You are much braver than I'd expected." He said as he leaned down to help me back up. Unsure if he meant it as an insult, a compliment, or both, I chose to let it go. Considering what had just transpired, it simply wasn't worth thinking about at that moment.

Most of the Warriors now moved ahead leaving Tadeo and me with only a few men trailing behind us.

"Why are…" I stopped myself, realizing I could never remember the names he'd said earlier. "…those goddesses following us?" Question upon question crowded to the forefront of my mind. "Where am I?" As I spoke, I decided I must be dreaming.

"Mictecacihuatl and Coyolxauhuqui," his infectious smile caused me to blush.

As we continued walking into the city, we could hear ceremonial drumming and chanting. It grew louder as I attempted to determine the direction of its origin.

"I will tell you as much as I can, later. Right now, we need to get into formation," he said as he and I took the lead and the Warriors followed.

Puzzled by what I was witnessing, I asked in a low voice, "Tadeo, where are we?"

Tadeo didn't break stride. He spoke in hushed tones from behind his mask.

"We're in the Aztec capital, Tenochtitlan."

We paused as several richly dressed dignitaries being carried on litters and surrounded by a large retinue passed in front of us.

"That is the Emperor's family. Today a bloodletting ritual will be performed."

I noticed his clenched jawline through the side of his mask, as he fell silent.

"What does that mean?" I continued.

"Silence now! You will displease the gods with all this questioning." I had noticed an ancient temple in the distance earlier, and now as we approached it, I could see crowds of ornately dressed people surrounding it.

The clamor grew louder by the moment as we approached the crowd, and I experienced a deep sense of confusion accompanied by a dull pain in my chest; anxiety I thought, as I purposely took long deep breaths in an attempt to calm my nerves.

Strategically placed fires blazed throughout the city, and beautiful earthenware pottery decorated the walkways. The geometrically designed buildings demonstrated impressive skill and artistry. The numerous canals were beyond belief, even rivaling Venice, but with a more rustic appeal.

In the distance, I could hear the sound of mournful wailing. It grew louder as we neared the temple, causing me to cringe a little. I noticed Tadeo casting glances in my direction.

Tadeo gave instructions in a native dialect. I wasn't exactly sure what the dialect could be. However, he proceeded to explain to me in plain English, that we were taking our positions for the ceremony on the steps of the temple as The Shorn Ones. I suspected this was part of whatever festivity was about to take place.

A priest led the procession, followed by the Emperor, the Emperors' family, and finally, the Shorn Ones were now in position. I had no idea what was happening as I searched my memory for various history lessons, and finally settled on Mesoamerican history; The Aztec Empire, of course! I recalled they spoke Nahuatl, a native dialect.

I was watching the priest's preparations when a cold realization came over me; I was about to witness a sacrifice, the ritualistic blood sacrifice of a human being.

"NO!" I shrieked inwardly and felt myself about to faint as Tadeo and a couple of the other warriors pressed in on me from all sides to shield me from the dignitaries and keep me standing upright.

An ominous voice spoke inside my head. *"Birth, death, and rebirth...all is destroyed, one will choose...born again through sacrifice, the cycle will end and bring forth a new age."*

I felt myself falling.

* * *

As I stood up cautiously, a dull pain throbbed behind my eyes. I looked around wondering where on earth I could be. Surely my dream had evolved into a nightmare, as the room I was in slowly came into focus.

The lighting was poor, but I could make out the adobe structure I now found myself in. I stumbled towards a doorway as a most delicious aroma lead me into the next room. A thin, medium height woman came into view. I swiped the back of my hand over my eyes in an attempt to see better, as I approached her.

Her dark hair was pinned up in braided whorls on the sides of her head. I was fascinated by her rapid hand movements as she skilfully assembled tortillas. At that moment, she turned and smiled broadly at me. I smiled back in relief.

The woman didn't speak, only motioned for me to sit on a low wooden stool in front of a stone table covered in dried mud. It was similar to one I'd seen in Pueblo, Colorado on a trip with my parents.

I sat, and the aroma of savory spices floated around me as she placed a pottery bowl filled with a dark substance on the table in front of me. She followed this with handmade tortillas on an earthenware plate, along with a steaming mug. As I lifted the mug, I recognized the smell; atole, a full-flavored hot drink made of corn masa, an unrefined brown sugar called piloncillo, cinnamon sticks, and vanilla beans.

I discovered I was starving and ate with gusto. Having enjoyed an exceptional meal, I was utterly content to watch the woman's steady fluid motions as she continued her artistry in the kitchen.

I glanced down at my clothes, deciding the woman

must have changed me, as I was now wearing a long linen skirt, with colorful hand stitched birds and flowers around the floor-length hem. The sleeveless, somewhat ill-fitting top was a lovely shade of jade which matched the jade bracelet dangling from my wrist. Several other pieces of gold jewelry accompanied the bracelet, and a pair of not so comfortable sandals adorned my feet.

My fashion critiquing was interrupted when I glanced up to discover Tadeo standing in the doorway.

"I see you're awake?" His deep voice sent a shiver up my spine.

I considered his question for a moment. Technically I was dreaming, wasn't I? But now I wasn't sure he knew this.

"Am I?" I said, hoping he had a sense of humor as the words left my lips.

"What happened at the temple must never happen again. Thank the gods you were standing in between my second in command and me, so no one detected your outburst! If you hadn't passed out, you could have posed a great risk to yourself. The Emperor and the Priest would not have shown mercy." His chiseled features seemed more prominent without the face paint, I noted as he scolded me.

My eyes skimmed over his chest area, slightly exposed through his neck ornament. His skin looked perfectly smooth, his abs well-shaped and defined. A loincloth covered only his most intimate parts. I concluded the last revelation made me more uncomfortable than it did him. I was suddenly grateful for the poor lighting as I'm sure I was blushing.

A commotion outside interrupted my thoughts and Tadeo swiftly exited. I hesitantly started to follow, but the woman stopped me, shaking her head firmly. I hadn't even had the chance to ask him what her name was.

I pointed at my own chest with a smile and said, "Viviana."

The woman smiled back, pointing at her own chest, "Magda." Then she promptly went back to her work.

I paced around the two rooms and soon decided they were someone's living quarters, although to whom they belonged I didn't know. I was engrossed in scrutinizing an exquisitely designed headpiece to pass the time when a voice spoke close to my ear, and I jumped nervously.

"It's not one I personally treasure, but Magda keeps it around. Out of my esteem for her, I don't question it," He said in his deep voice.

Immediately I turned to face him. It finally dawned on me, this was Tadeo's dwelling.

"I'm glad to see you've returned. Maybe now you can start answering some of my questions. First off, am I still in Tenochtitlan?" I demanded.

Tadeo's posture was more at ease as he leaned on the adobe wall, hands behind him, and his voice calm.

"I apologize. You've been unconscious." He trailed off before continuing. "This mission... It's impossible.

I don't know what the gods were thinking. But who am I to question them?" He turned and paced toward the opposite wall, his calm demeanor now replaced by tension. He opened the wooden shutters to allow natural light into the room.

"Yes, you are still in Tenochtitlan. Well, kind of. You are dream traveling here so your spirit can take on its natural form while you are here. We refer to it as Yalhua which means yesterday in Nahuatl. It's complicated. I'm not even sure I understand completely. But listen, we don't have time to discuss this right now. Those were guards who came just now to warn me of a possible breach of the barrier around the sacred grounds, which protect the city." He looked me dead in the eyes as if speaking to my soul, "We will be joining the rest of the warriors now."

His perfectly shaped eyebrows accented his mysterious deep brown eyes, as his tousled hair framed his handsome face. The fear of what he'd just said was eased somewhat by the tone of his voice, as I once again followed him into the unknown.

CHAPTER TWO

I slowly pulled myself up in bed, staring blankly out the window as Mamá drew back the curtains. *Another one of my bizarre dreams,* was all I could think as I sat there trying to clear the cobwebs and motivate myself to get up.

Mamá moved briskly to my side and leaned over to give me a breezy kiss on the forehead. Out of the corner of my eye, I could see it was another overcast day in the Pacific Northwest. Oh, yay, I told myself sarcastically, as my body strongly objected to getting up so early.

The loving look in Mamá's eyes sent warmth straight to my heart as she smiled at me then breezed out saying, "Time to get up sleepyhead."

Minutes later the hot spray of the shower was

caressing my body like a soothing massage. The steam allowed my thoughts to drift, as I doused my loofah with aromatic shower gel.

As I spread the rich, creamy lather over my body, the memory of my recurring dream returned, ruining my fun shower experience. I finished up quickly, while details of the dreams weighed heavily on my mind; *what exactly did they mean, if anything?*

As I reached the bottom of the back staircase, I heard a familiar voice; the strong accent, soft and deep and eloquent, especially when speaking English, could only be one person, my uncle, Humberto.

It had been two years since we'd seen each other. The last time had been in Mexico, in my mother's home state of Zacatecas celebrating my Quinceañera; my fifteenth birthday. My parents had agreed to host the event there since I spent so little time with that side of our family.

The day had been perfect, magical almost until I found my father, uncle Humberto, and another gentleman I didn't know, in a heated debate. They were standing in an arched corridor covered in Bugambilias with their vibrant magenta colored flowers, next to a maze of Pitaya cactus on my grandfather's ranch.

The conversation was intense though I was unable to hear the details. When they noticed my presence, they disbanded quickly, leaving only my father to derail me from what I had semi-witnessed.

Before I could inquire, my Dad was already

speaking to me.

"My sweet girl, please don't be alarmed with the slight difference of opinions we were having. We are not always going to agree with others, but we must find common grounds to understand each other respectfully." He smiled and took my arm in his, sweeping me off my feet for an impromptu father-daughter dance.

That was the last time I'd seen my Uncle Humberto. The man who was like my second father. He'd vanished from my life, without a word, until today.

Now as I approached him quietly his back was to me, but I noticed him pushing his cell phone into the inner pocket of his tailored blazer. Mamá stood off to one side looking at him admiringly.

Caught up with staring at Mamá, I was surprised when Uncle Humberto suddenly turned to face me. There he was, tall, lean, golden tanned skin, sun-kissed hair and the beautiful hazel eyes that seemed to be a staple in the Villareal family. Just as handsome as ever.

"Viviana!" He exclaimed, pulling me into his embrace as both our eyes filled with tears. I could feel his heart thumping as we both wept silently. Once again, I felt the safety of his strong arms. It was all I needed to forgive him for his absence for the past two years. They had been the most difficult years of my life. It just seemed that my uncle, my best friend, had abandoned me.

I sensed my mother's gaze, perhaps wondering if

we'd remembered she was there as we had our moment together. He must've felt it too as he slowly released me, caressing my cheek, and bestowing his beautiful smile on me.

"Uncle Humberto, how are you?" I said, in a weak attempt to sound mature.

Once again, his arm encircled my waist, this time leading me toward the breakfast room. "I've missed you so much, my dear." His voice trailed off into an emotional silence which we both understood.

Attempting to change the mood, he said, "How gorgeous and grown up you've grown my child."

I accepted the compliment graciously, "You're much too kind Uncle Humberto."

Knowing I had school ahead of me, I engaged only in small talk over coffee and lemon scones. I would've allowed for more but felt pressed for time.

Rising from the table I opened the French doors, clutching the handles as I closed my eyes, allowing the fresh morning air to flow into my lungs. The ghostly sun peeking through the fog caused me sudden pangs as memories of morning jogs with Mamá in the misty morning air stirred in my head. I quickly retreated, exchanging a few more words before announcing my departure.

That day, the Seattle morning felt mild, probably in the fifties but it was overcast and certainly looked like more rain was on the way, as I approached the waiting car.

"Viviana, please wait," Humberto said as he rushed

to my side, causing me to stop and allow him to catch up.

He handed me a little brown suede satchel. I peeked in and pulled out a gorgeous Aztec sundial pendant, hanging from a delicate diamond cut gold chain. I felt a strange energy emanating from the pendant, as a light breeze caressed my skin.

"Thank you, uncle Humberto, it's so beautiful," I said, realizing the pendant reminded me of the tattoo Tadeo wore in my dreams. It seemed the dreams were never far from my thoughts.

Humberto, pleased with my reaction proceeded to explain, "I had intended to give it to you the last time we saw each other, at your Quinceañera. I've kept it with me this entire time, it made me feel connected to you in a small way."

I had to admit to myself, that made absolutely no sense, but I just smiled.

He continued to observe me carefully as if he were trying to read my mind. I shook off the feeling and continued toward the car, waving goodbye as I slid into the back seat.

The car's interior was all porcelain and black leather with carbon fiber and black piano lacquer wood trim. My mother's choice. She always loved the finer niceties in life.

Jim, our driver, greeted me and ushered me into the back closing the door behind me. He then got behind the wheel to drive me to school.

"So, how did you like your surprise?" He asked

smiling at me in the rear-view mirror, as he pulled out of the circular driveway.

He was the only person I'd confided in during the last two years, about my longing for my uncle Humberto and our conversations.

I quickly returned his smile as I carefully considered how to answer him. Mentally, it was fun having my uncle back. Perhaps the lapse of time made it a bit awkward, but there was something different about our encounter this time.

"Surprised, that's for sure. It's nice to have my uncle back." I said, contemplating what those words meant to me.

We arrived at the Jesuit Preparatory Academy, a private all-girls Catholic school. I'd attended the same school since the seventh grade. A boarding school, technically. But a few, including myself, didn't board there. It was one of the privileges most teenagers with my family's means could boast about, but I found it meaningless.

Jim opened my door, and we knuckle bumped, a routine we'd maintained since I was in grade school. He sent me off with a "Go get'em Becks!" nicknaming me after David Beckham, the English footballer I'd obsessed over as a child.

I wondered if other chauffeurs had special greetings and farewells for their client's kids?

I was a footballer, also known as a soccer player. Most of my friends and I played in a year-round soccer club, but during the high school season, we'd take a break and play for our schools as standard practice.

I believed myself to be a decent player, maybe not as finessed as some, but what I lacked in skills and fancy footwork, I made up for in speed and aggressiveness. Even the latter tended to elude me, as of late. Maybe it was the fact that I was seldom able to get a full night's rest, but ever since I'd started having the strange dreams, I'd had a crappy attitude on the pitch.

As I made my way to the top of the front steps, I heard someone behind me greet Miss Davenport, our dreadful headmistress. Although I don't believe she consumes alcohol, there is something about her that reminds me of Miss Hannigan in Annie, which makes me want to break out singing 'It's a hard knock life,' not for me, but for her.

Miss Davenport always seemed to show contempt towards the students. She was so grim all the time. I just couldn't understand why she was at the school if she disliked teaching so much.

"Good morning Miss Magnus…Miss Anderson." Her monotone voice just as aloof as her attitude; the headmistress was simply too much. But not as much as Zoe Anderson and her mean streak, who was apparently right behind me.

Zoe is an excellent swimmer, captain of the school's swim team and all-round tough girl. We'd gone to school together since preschool. Our fathers were friends through the business they've conducted together, over the years. Therefore, it was sometimes difficult to avoid her in social settings.

As she walked past me, I caught a glimpse of her disapproving glare. Sudden anger overcame me as she smirked and barged past me. Trying hard to control my temper I took deep breaths. It seemed the deeper I breathed, the tighter my chest became as if it would burst. Sometimes it was impossible dealing with her.

"What's wrong Viv? At a loss for words?" She snickered, as I was forced to take the higher ground, remaining as calm as possible. I would be damned if I would give her the chance to wreak havoc on my mood. I walked right past her, not giving her a second thought.

Mr. Caberletti the Theology / Foundations in Faith professor was a quiet average size middle-aged man. An Italian native, he had studied at the Pontifical Georgian University in Rome. A Catholic Bishop Emeritus, in other words, a bishop without a parish or diocese who by his own request had been laicized, which I understood to be very rare. No longer required to live a life of celibacy, he was a layperson, and the question remained, why? Why would he have requested laicization? No one seemed to know the answer to that question.

"Miss Magnus…Miss Magnus?" He was shaking his head at me. "Welcome back to class. I would appreciate it if you'd refrain from falling asleep in here again," he said as he frowned at me.

"I apologize, Mr. Caberletti, sir. Please be assured it will not happen again." I hadn't even finished speaking when I heard a distinct chuckle to my left. I turned to find the perpetrator. It was Zoe, challenging me with a scornful look.

My body temperature rose suddenly, as a sick feeling washed over me. Mr. Caberletti must've still been looking at me as he quickly sprang into action. He was at my side in a moment feeling my forehead with the back of his hand.

"Dear child you're burning up. You must be coming down with something."

The classroom seemed to close in on me as I felt deprived of oxygen and started hyperventilating. The pain in my head was like a vice closing tightly, and my eyes were burning. I could barely hear the slight commotion of hushed whispers as if they were coming from a distance. "All right class, please remain calm and stay seated."

Without warning, a set of arms swept me off my feet, pulling me in tightly as I was carried swiftly toward what I assumed was the infirmary. Then everything became muddled and went dark.

No one noticed when I awoke, so I kept my eyes closed as I tried to wrap my thoughts around what had just happened. My father and Uncle Humberto were at my side, but strangely, Mamá was not.

How long had I been out? Where was I?

Henry James Magnus, my father, was an astute businessman. Although he came from a wealthy family, there was no questioning his business sense. There also was no questioning his love for me. I'd always believed there were no secrets between us, but as I listened in on his and Humberto's conversation, I realized they were quietly talking about me.

My mind started spinning as I overheard their conversation.

"She needs to know the truth now, Henry. It's time. No matter how terrifying this seems to you, we need to trust her with this information and believe she will be able to handle it as well as anyone could. It's not like we have a choice anymore," Humberto said. I could sense his pacing. "I'm going to the Tlatcani, so take your pick; tell her, or the council of the Calpulli will do so."

There was a brief silence followed by the opening and closing of a door, as I lay puzzling over the meaning of my uncle's threat.

Unsure if I should continue pretending to be out, or start probing my father, I felt a strange, powerful force. It seemed to be lurking within me, waiting.

The door opened again, and I listened as faint footsteps came to a stop at my side. Someone took one of my hands into their own.

"Has she awakened?" spoke a voice I clearly recognized.

My father, who had apparently remained in the room, inhaled deeply before he responded.

"No, not yet, but I suspect she will at any moment." adding something under his breath. "I don't think it is wise that she finds you in here when she wakes. I will call you when she does, once I've had an opportunity to speak to her. Then you can do what you must."

I froze in fear at his words. *Why is Zoe Anderson here, and what is my father keeping from me?* I wanted badly to open my eyes, but I waited for Zoe to exit the room.

Slowly I opened my eyes and took in my surroundings. It wasn't the infirmary, but I did recognize it as one of the private suites in the dorm. *Perhaps Mr. Caberletti couldn't make it to the infirmary? But then what is it Zoe needs to do?*

"Dad?" I said to get his attention, and he rushed to my side.

"How are you, my sweet girl? You had us worried for a while there," His smile was warm and friendly.

"I'm – I'm not sure what happened?" I said as I attempted to scoot myself up in the bed.

He hurried to assist me with an arm under my shoulders.

"I got it, Dad."

The expression on his face was one of pained concern as if begging me to at least allow him to father me. It had been like this over the past few months, I continued to allow my stubbornness to take over and avoid any sign of weakness on my part.

"What's wrong Dad?" I said as I stood up, a bit lightheaded. I shook it off as I walked toward the large window overlooking the beautiful courtyard. There was a gargoyle to the right of the window which I swore was grinning at me.

"I was worried. Mr. Caberletti said you weren't

quite yourself this morning; falling asleep in class, and he thought you had a fever." I could see a glint of a tear in his eyes. Upon closer inspection, he looked a bit flustered and unkempt.

Dad sighed deeply, pacing around the room and rubbing the back of his neck. I'd seen this look on him only a couple of times before; it was usually followed by something I didn't want to hear.

My handsome father had aged. There were subtle crow's feet at the corners of his eyes. His forehead bore the beginnings of deep wrinkles. Henry Magnus had become thinner.

To anyone else, the effects of aging would weigh them down. But on my father, his features seemed enhanced by them. His light olive complexion, dark brown hair, and lean build still demanded attention, though he'd never been one to seek it, only having eyes for my mother. Where was Mamá anyway?

I looked around the room searching for her, noticing his hands clenched at his sides, knuckles white, and sadness in his eyes. He knew precisely what my eyes sought.

"You know Viviana, I miss her as well…everything reminds me of her, especially you. But this needs to stop!" His raised voice shocked me. He caught his breath. "I've made every possible attempt to help you, us, to get through this. But you have to help me here."

A chill came over me, all I wanted to do was run away, but he held me tightly.

"She's not coming back. You know that. You must

let her go, Sweetie. It's time," he whispered.

Burying my face in his broad shoulder, I inhaled his familiar scent of salt air and ocean water. I wanted desperately to go back to dreaming. I couldn't handle this.

She's dead, and she's never coming back. Be strong they said.

I was trying. But I was losing a fight against a ghost...

R. CASTRO

CHAPTER THREE

Sporadic Fatal Insomnia. I'd come to learn about the rare sleep disorder and to hate it.

Less than two years ago, my mother started suffering from sleep deprivation, which led to panic attacks and strange phobias along with exaggerated hallucinations.

The specialists were baffled and at first, couldn't find what led to her inability to sleep.

Mamá objected strenuously to my father about undergoing further testing. She started to deteriorate rapidly and became unresponsive. It was only then that her medical team diagnosed her. Unfortunately, even the specialists with all their combined degrees could not explain why she'd developed such a rare condition, as the patterns weren't consistent. She often had bruising that appeared in random places on her body.

Early on she experienced vivid dreams whenever she occasionally slept. When the sleeping stopped, the hallucinations and panic attacks increased, causing her to lose her entire perspective of reality slowly but surely.

She would tremble with difficulty speaking and scream at whatever her depraved mind would make up; sometimes, requiring us to hold her down. Her nightmares were always about fire.

Against all the medical advice, my father kept her home until the day she became comatose.

I rode with her in the ambulance as she was transported the short distance to the hospital. I watched her nervously, not knowing it would be her final day. I still believed there was something the doctors could do.

"Sir, with all due respect, put your medical degree aside. What would you do if that was your wife!" Papa shouted. I could hear someone asking him to calm down and lower his voice.

"Mr. Magnus, please lower your voice. Your outburst isn't going to get any of us to respond any faster. If anything, it's going to get you escorted out by security. I do understand your frustrations, but we are doing all we can at the moment."

There was a silence, as I continued watching over Mamá.

"Very well." His voice a bit calmer, but I knew full

well what it meant. He was not happy. The edge in his tone was lethal.

I sat quietly by her side that last day, wondering if her mind and body were finally getting their much-needed rest. At that very moment, I had a supernatural experience, right there by my mother's side. I was carefully tucking her hair behind her ears, when a mist formed out of nowhere, hovering over me. I peered cautiously at it, even waved my hand through it, sensing there was a force of some kind within it. Startled but intrigued I had no time to react as the mist settled over Mamá's body. I barely heard the loud beeping when the medical team rushed in, pushing me out of the room.

She died. The mist had come for her. It wasn't there to perform some miracle. It was there to take her away from me at the tender age of sixteen.

The day's immediately following her death were full of emptiness, as I went completely numb. I grew tired of those who tried to tell me to be strong or even explain death as temporary, and how we'd be together again. I lashed out. I didn't care.

My mom had been an active member or our church, filling many stewardship roles. Her so-called friends had gradually abandoned her, not wanting to take the time to understand her rare disease. Abandoning her to her fate.

They usually feigned concern when my father was around. They offered their support to him. Of course, they did. His money made an impact.

Slowly, I became embittered towards most of our church friends, as I viewed their hypocrisy from a distance. They were ever so quick to show their "caring" nature when it would be noticed. Their charitable contributions, whether in time or money, were not so philanthropic, as they were deceitful acts of self-righteousness.

There was one lady, however, who was a real friend to my mother and our family. Because of her genuine kindness, I never lost faith in my spiritual beliefs, only in the self-declared "leaders" within the religious structure that was the church.

Miss Mandy taught me you don't always have to bring anything but your true love and friendship to make a difference to another person. Conversation and companionship are often all a person needs to get through the day; someone who cares without an ulterior motive. She'd sat with my mom doing her needlework, discussing any and every topic that seemed to pique Mamá's interest. Simply sitting there, quietly in her presence was often all Mamá needed. Just a reminder that she too was still there.

Dad came to the same inescapable conclusion, as we drifted away from the church after Mamá passed. When his tithing stopped, several "concerned" members were quickly at his side "offering" nurturing support.

Where had they been through our most trying times? Always in the distance, and only helping where their contributions would be conspicuous.

No, my father was not an idiot, and neither was I.

I came to understand why so many people left their churches. It wasn't necessarily the scriptures that pushed them away, it was the people.

My strange dreams started about a week after Mamá's death. I would always awake from these exhausted. They seemed to magnify the pain of her death. So much so I often thought I could hear her come into my room in the mornings. It was a comforting feeling that soon turned to melancholy.

I started to sense her around me everywhere. Often I was unable to separate truth from fantasy. So many memories ran through me, causing me to believe she was still a part of my life in some strange way. It just seemed easier that way.

Dad tried reasoning with me and even sent me to therapists. But my denial helped to keep me functioning.

I knew I'd need to accept her passing; it wasn't a choice. I just needed to hold onto her a little longer. I realized how devastating it must have been for my father; to see his only child drowning in grief.

I closed my eyes allowing her memory to fill me. Her sweet morning kisses, the agony of her early departure. The tears rolled down my face, landing directly over my heart.

You will always be with me, Mamá. I love you for all eternity. I whispered it to the air as I finally released her from the false reality I'd created.

Bye Mamá.

CHAPTER FOUR

With Mamá *gone nothing matters anymore*, I thought as I pulled my hair out of its tight bun, allowing it to flow freely down my back.

Accepting reality was painful and left me feeling cold and empty. Slowly, however, a fierce core of warmth was growing deep down inside me that I couldn't explain.

I sensed someone in the room behind me at that moment and spun around to find myself staring at Zoe.

She was leaning against the mahogany floor to ceiling bookcase, her arms crossed over her chest, and her long jet black hair pulled over one shoulder. Her eyes glittered like obsidian as she watched me with a bemused expression.

I felt anger rising within but managed to maintain my composure.

"What are you doing here and where is my father?" I demanded as I headed for the door.

Pain shot through my hand as I grabbed the door handle. It was as if I had taken hold of a shard of ice. I let out an involuntary gasp.

I shot an accusing look at Zoe. "Did you do that?"

"You're going to have a lot of questions, naturally." She said calmly, as she approached me. I noticed she was no longer wearing her school uniform.

The royal blue top highlighted her beautiful shoulders and complimented her trim figure. Her distressed, skinny jeans, were paired with white leather espadrille flats. The rose color on her lips was a perfect contrast to her pale skin. Zoe managed to make a basic look, absolutely lethal. She was truly stunning.

"Get changed and let's get out of here. We're going for a ride. I'll tell you everything I know on the way. Your dad and the others will catch up with us later." She quietly summoned whatever magic she possessed, and the door handle returned to room temperature.

I couldn't help wondering about the phenomenon I'd just witnessed.

As we sped north on Interstate 5, I asked, "Can you give me some idea where we're headed?"

"Sacred tribal grounds where we can't be followed," was her terse reply.

The words from my dreams suddenly flooded back

as a reminder of Tadeo and his reference to sacred grounds and being followed. I listened for thundering sounds in the distance and shifted nervously in my seat as the landscape flashed by the window.

We were going to the Lummi Indian Reservation.

Sensing my unease, Zoe began to tell me a story. But not just any story as it turned out, it was the creation story.

"Have you heard of the Legend of the Five Suns?" She asked, as once again she checked her mirrors. "The Ometecuhtli/Omecihuatl was the original god/goddess; good and bad, chaos and order, light and darkness, motion and stillness, male and female. This god of duality, Lord of Life, created four children, who were also gods. They each represented one of the four directions; Xipe Totec – north, Huitzilopochtli – south, Quetzalcoatl – East, and Tezcatlipoca – west."

I recognized the names from the native Nahuatl language, the language I'd heard in my dreams.

"The Aztec's believed their empire was the very center of the universe. Therefore, directions were vital to them." She continued, as she signaled and changed lanes to pass.

"The Four Gods created water and other gods, then waged war using their other godly creations. It's how Mictlantecutli or Mictlan, the God of Death and the underworld came into being. I had to research most of this online via the Aztec-History website." As I listened, I was trying to comprehend how all this fit in with my dreams.

"The Four Gods knew a great source of energy would be needed to sustain life on the earth they'd created, but to build such power would require a great sacrifice of one of their own, and thus the sun was formed of godly sacrifices. However, creating a sun proved to be challenging." She continued to explain, "The first three attempts by the god patrons failed, I guess one could chalk it up to lack of experience. The fourth attempt was made by a female god, who was the sister of the Third Sun, who had been struck down by Tezcatlipoca and Quetzalcoatl in a jealous rage. The earth was once again destroyed, causing the Four Gods to recreate it once again. This is the earth that still exists today. The Fourth Sun's name was Calchiuhtlicue or Nahui Atl."

Zoe took a deep breath before continuing, but I noticed a shift in the tone of her voice.

"The Fifth Sun, which followed the re-creation of the earth, represented earthquakes. The proud, pompous god, Tecuciztecatl offered himself as the patron. But it was the humble god Nanahuatzin whom the gods preferred. He'd proven himself valiant, jumping into the great fire when Tecuciztecatl was too afraid. Enraged upon witnessing this, Tecuciztecatl jumped in the fire as well, creating two suns. The gods knew they couldn't leave the earth with two suns, so they threw a rabbit at the second sun, causing its light to go dim, thus, creating the moon."

Having shared the legend, Zoe fell silent, eyes fixed on the road ahead, as I digested what she'd just told me. I was pretty foggy as to what it all meant, but I knew I was somehow going to be a participant in it.

"Tecuciztecatl, we refer to as the Moon God, Nanahuatzin the Sun, and Nahui Atl – The Fourth Sun, as the Lady of the Jade Skirts." She added, and I was reminded, yet again, of my dreams and the jade bracelet.

Pushing the thoughts aside, we zoomed past the Tulalip Indian Reservation. I wondered what was different about the Lummi Reservation, that we had to travel further.

"The Moon God wants final revenge on the Sun, to regain his pride and position among the higher gods. He's called on two of the most psychotic goddesses, Mictecacihuatl of the underworld and Coyolxauhqui his companion goddess of the moon to exact his revenge. I call them Micteca and Coyolxa because these Aztec deity names are a mouthful." Zoe smiled wryly at me.

Behind us, in the distance, I could see an ominous dark cloud forming.

"The Moon God wants a battle on earth to prevent the next sacrifice which happens every fifty-two years. He plans on creating four lunar eclipses, four blood moons, each one signifying death." She broke off the conversation, with a shocked look on her face, as the threatening cloud came into her line of sight. It was evident she read more into the cloud than I did but she pressed on.

"The gods had anticipated the Moon God's

outrage, so they formulated The Tetrad Prophecy of the Four Blood Moons. The gods will not come to earth to fight the battle for the humans. Instead, they provided the Pillar of Life, which holds the Five Pendants of Creation. These pendants are now scattered around the earth, and can only be retrieved by the Elemental Linx, the new generation of earth gods and goddesses with superior elemental powers." She trailed off.

I stared at Zoe remembering the shift in her eyes and the icy door handle. *Was she one of these Elemental Linx she spoke of?*

"The gods appointed keepers called the Calpulli to oversee the prophecy and ensure that it is fulfilled. This ancient order is tasked with providing the blood sacrifice to the Sun which is performed every fifty-two years, so the Sun doesn't fall from the sky." The corners of her mouth turned upward in a faint smile. "Also, as the guardians of the prophecy, they are responsible for the protection of the Linx."

"It is foretold in prophecy that the earth's destruction will come in the form of volcanic eruptions and massive earthquakes if the Linx fail to stop the Moon God," Zoe explained.

"Zoe, I'm sorry. This all seems almost comical, but somehow, I know you're telling me the truth, and that scares me. How do you and I fit into all this? And my father?" I broke off as the cloud we'd seen earlier came into full view as we rounded a bend.

The trouble is, it wasn't precisely a cloud, per se,

but a giant serpent in the sky slithering its way towards us.

Zoe floored the gas pedal of her Alfa Romeo Coupe, and we rocketed forward.

A white sports car that seemed to come out of the cloud quickly wove its way through traffic behind us. I felt the vibration of thunder reverberate through the sky. Lightning reflected off the black hood of the car, sending chills through me.

"My dad better get me a faster car after this. That's a flippin' McLaren 675LT. I don't know if I can outrun it," she said, focusing on the road, with only a brief glance in the rear-view mirror. "Can you feel the energy coming from that car? Whoever is in there is manipulating that cloud."

She explained the specs of the car to me, which I assumed was an attempt to settle her nerves while doing a darn good job of putting my own on edge. Panic rose in me, as I felt agitation and fear combined.

I turned to see the car right behind us, while Zoe changed lanes quickly. The windows of the McLaren were tinted so dark I could see nothing but what looked like a pair of glowing blue eyes staring right at me.

There was a clear stretch of road ahead. *Surely, we're done for*, I thought, as the white car got even closer to us.

With no warning, Zoe suddenly exited the freeway onto an access road. I grabbed for the leather grab handle above the window with my right hand and the bottom of the red leather trimmed bucket seat with the other.

The McLaren driver hadn't anticipated the move, but as we sped underneath the freeway I noticed the other car slam into reverse, smoke pouring from its tires. In a matter of seconds, it was descending the ramp we'd just taken.

Zoe made another left turn onto a straight, narrow road. The ocean came into view, and the strange black cloud gradually dissipated behind us as the McLaren pulled over and stopped, no longer pursuing us.

As soon as the McLaren was out of sight, Zoe pulled over on the narrow shoulder of the road. Visibly shaken she exited the car and slid to a seated position on the ground. I ran to her side.

We sat in complete silence leaning against the car, as the ocean waves broke against the shore.

Breathing deeply, Zoe pushed her fingers through her glossy hair.

"When your mom died, I wanted nothing more than to reach out to you." She fought back tears, as an icy breath escaped her and she bit down on her lower lip.

"I can feel a person's emotions shift. Perhaps one of the so-called gifts I don't much enjoy." She waved off the question I was dying to ask, motioning me to wait. "You were in so much pain, I didn't know how to approach you. Each time I tried, I was torn, feeling what you were going through and I couldn't cope with it." She pushed her hair away from her face as she stared into the distance through tearful eyes.

"Viv, I get it. Why you couldn't let go...of your mom."

The pain, the struggle was all way too much. I jumped to my feet. I paid no heed to how sharp my words were.

"Zoe, don't go there! You have no right! Please, just stop." A tug of reason from within forced me to pull it together. My words turned to whispers as my trembling hand pointed to my heart. "You can't possibly imagine..." My words petered out.

Shaken by the thoughts flooding through my mind I started walking in the direction we'd been headed. My d'Orsay black patent and suede flats wouldn't have been my first choice for the task, but they were still better than my school shoes.

The ocean breezes reached me in small lingering gusts as I inhaled deeply of the salty air.

I heard Zoe get in the car, the sound of the revving engine danced in my mind. I was paying no attention when she pulled up beside me.

"Get in." She called out to me, and I complied.

She reached for the knob on the front control panel, turning up the heat. The corners of her mouth trembled; she was cold, I could tell.

"I was young when my element first appeared to me," she let out a soft laugh. "I never really opened up to anyone. My father would just tell everyone I suffered from nightmares."

Raising her right hand from the steering wheel, she summoned an orb of water that circled above the surface of her palm; swirling so beautifully before it froze, then vanished seconds later.

She explained how her father had encouraged her to block it out as much as she could, and was quick to dismiss her as a mere child.

"Viv, you've always had a loving, caring family." She inhaled deeply. "My father was the absentee dad. I'm sure being a single parent wasn't easy, but I reminded him of something he wasn't prepared to face, so he avoided me. I imagine it was kind of like what you've been going through," she said, avoiding eye contact. "I'm not saying this looking for a pity party. I just want you to understand where this is going. Why I couldn't get close to you. You're not the only one hurting." She stared straight at me, and I watched as her eyes transformed once again into obsidian crystals.

Stroking her long gorgeous dark hair, she returned her focus to the road, moving to the right to allow an approaching vehicle to pass.

She cleared her throat as she continued. "The McLaren that was on our tail was no coincidence. There are higher forces at play here, more than any mere human can imagine."

Zoe explained how my father came to her aid back when she was ten, causing me to smile warmly thinking about his kind nature. I became completely engrossed in her story, how our fathers were part of the Calpulli and she had this extraordinary elemental gift of water that filled her with purpose. Her words mingled with my thoughts as I attempted to make a connection with what I'd been experiencing myself.

CHAPTER FIVE

Zoe brought the car to a halt at the head of a trail that led down to the shore. Pulled up on the sand were four large wooden canoes, and on the beach, a couple of dozen men gathered around five bonfires. The central fire pit was the largest and circling each fire were two dancers dressed in black, with exotic headpieces, depicting birds with massive beaks. Four drummers supplied the rhythm and one individual chanted in a native tongue.

Most impressive of all were the carved wooden statues and a totem pole, all painted in bright colors.

We descended a flight of steep stairs and approached the central circle. I felt lightheaded, as I focused on the waves breaking on the beach. A gust of wind forced a euphoric combination of ocean breeze and smoke through my airways, infusing my mind.

Zoe dropped to her knees, raising her hands to the sky, and began swaying rhythmically from side to side in time with the chanting.

Some serious questions were welling up in my mind, but I was being calmed by an invisible force within.

The men formed a large circle around us, as the masked dancers shuffled back and forth within the circle. I surrendered myself to the rhythmic chant and the motions of the dance.

There must've been something hallucinogenic in the fires because Zoe seemed to be parting the overcast sky, swaying her hands in the air as if conducting a great symphony.

The sun peeked through, lighting and bringing sharp clarity to everything it touched. As it caressed my skin, the warmth drew me closer to the source, that massive star in the sky.

The sun's rays illuminated the totem pole, and my heartbeat became synchronized with the drums.

My entire body was aglow. *It must be a combination of the sun's intense rays and the smoke*, I decided. Giving in to the chanting I dropped to my knees on the sand. Wrapping my arms around myself, I curled up in a fetal position letting the sand cradle my body. I felt my emotions rise with a fury I'd never experienced before, pushing away the tedium of life. *Preoccupation with nonsense has become a drug to humans, veiling any perspective of actual meaning or identity.*

The drums and the chanting filled my senses, but the static of life continued to haunt me until I heard a cry coming from somewhere deep inside me. I wrapped my arms around myself even tighter.

Waves crashed upon the shore and the rain pelted down. A strong wind pushed its way through like an uninvited guest. My heart raced, and I was too afraid to open my eyes.

I tried to convince myself that fairy tales don't exist, not even the scary ones. *We are all inherently good, but at some point, we make a choice. Will we be consumed by good or evil, light or darkness?* I thought as I dug deep inside, trusting myself, searching for the light, my hope, some self-forgiveness. The realization and acceptance brought me a deep feeling of peace.

Suddenly, everything came to a stop. All that could be heard was the crackling of the fires and the sizzling as raindrops evaporated in the flames. I opened my eyes to find everyone just standing stock still and staring at me. I fought to compose myself and rose to my feet.

An older slightly overweight man stepped forward and began to speak. "We are the Lhaq'temish 'People of the Sea.'" "This is a healing ceremony for you, as you have been troubled. The Great Spirit cannot help you ascend until you can find the inner peace needed for your rebirth. We have fulfilled our part, and now it is time for you to rise to your higher purpose."

As one, the entire assembly turned and walked towards the water. They climbed into the canoes and paddled away in unison until they were out of sight.

Looking around me I discovered Zoe sitting on a log which had washed up on the beach. She seemed devoid of emotion. A bit glazed myself I sat down next to her. We continued to sit there, not speaking, for a long time.

Finally, from up the beach, I noticed a figure walking decisively in our direction. As he neared I could see it was a young man of about our own age; his steps were unfaltering. The red of his shirt was in sharp contrast with his bright blue eyes. The warm brown hair that framed his face displayed light caramel hues. His tall, slender body was lightly tanned.

Suddenly Zoe was pulling on my arm. In a low voice, she said. "Let's go. Something doesn't feel right about this guy."

I couldn't keep my eyes off him, as I followed her up the steps.

When we reached the top, we discovered the white McLaren blocking Zoe's car.

A sudden feeling of being hunted caused my body temperature to rise. Unlike at other times, though, I suddenly felt in control and unafraid. Boldness overtook me as I allowed my fire element to ignite within me.

I parted my lips in a mischievous smile, granting the inner flame permission to build freely within me; ready to do my bidding.

As the guy continued to approach us, I studied him carefully. He flashed me an impertinent smile. The clouds swirled in the sky, pulling lower as if in salutation. *It's his response to my flame*, I realized.

Zoe stepped forward, motioning the clouds away with a simple flick of her wrist. Her scornful look sent a blistering chill through the air, as she conjured a blade of ice. It slammed into the ground in front of him, forcing him to stop in his tracks.

From behind us came the sound of one pair of hands clapping, as my flame recoiled.

Ice blue eyes, thick dark eyebrows with matching dark wavy hair belonged to the most perfect human male I'd ever set eyes on. He was leaning against the white McLaren.

The coloring in my face betrayed me as Zoe took the lead and stepped forward.

"Who are you and why are you following us?" She demanded as we moved swiftly to the other side of her car. The guy from the beach reached the top of the landing, moving with a bit of a swagger towards the white car.

The screeching of tires shattered the silence as a silver Mercedes came into view, locking its brakes, and sliding to a stop, boxing in the McLaren.

I knew the car and its driver.

Jim remained in the driver's seat, while the two back doors swung open as my father and Mr. Anderson – Zoe's dad emerged. Just as I was about to move again, a red Audi A8 pulled in, my mother's car, with Humberto at the wheel.

It took me a moment to compose myself, realizing it wasn't Mamá who'd come to my rescue, reminding myself she was never coming back.

CHAPTER SIX

I sensed an emotional intensity building in the air around Zoe. Waves of cold radiated from her body as I stepped cautiously around her and moved to join my father.

Humberto was now at the center of the gathering extending his hand to the older guy, who had stepped away from the McLaren to greet him. They exchanged some friendly shoulder patting, and he whispered something to Humberto which only served to further infuriate Zoe. Humberto then greeted the younger guy, who moved to embrace him.

Dad placed a hand on my shoulder protectively.

"Allow me to introduce Ollin," Humberto announced, with a playful jab to Ollin's ribs. He was the younger of the two, who'd made his appearance from the beach.

Ollin shook hands with my father and Mr. Anderson." It's a pleasure to meet you both."

He moved in Zoe's direction but thought better of it upon observing her body language. He chose instead to nod his head gracefully in each of our directions; a wise choice.

"I'm at a loss here. These two imbeciles tried to kill us with their road rage!" Zoe said coldly, quivering in anger. "So, what... they're friendlies now?"

Alasdair presented himself to our fathers formally. I caught him eyeing me as he shook their hands. He barely acknowledged Zoe and me, as my father presented him to us, "Zoe, Viviana, this is Alasdair, Ollin's brother."

Humberto interrupted the awkward moment. "Why don't we all move to Elder Thomas's home and take refuge for the evening?"

Mr. Anderson was about to climb in the car with his daughter, but Zoe said curtly," If you don't mind Dad I'd like Viviana to ride with me."

I was thankful for Zoe's quick thinking as we followed the Audi and Mercedes, while the McLaren followed us; allowing for a few minutes of privacy to question Zoe a little more.

"I'm still confused as to why we are here? What's with the welcome party, and now these two, who are they?" I pressed.

"I don't know about Alasdair. But Ollin is like us,

an elemental," she said, glancing in her rearview mirror at the car trailing behind us.

Zoe offered no further explanations as we proceeded a few miles along the shore to a modest blue house. The older gentleman from the beach, who'd spoken to me earlier, greeted us at the door and introduced himself as Elder Thomas. He and my father embraced warmly like old friends, then he stepped aside so the rest of us could pass. He and my dad exchanged pleasantries while clasping each other's hand warmly.

As we made our way through the small entrance and into the living space at the back, the large windows presented an unobstructed view of Puget Sound, Hales Passage & the San Juan Islands. The view was breathtaking. I knew these waterways from spending many weekends there on my dad's speedboat.

The evening sky was putting on quite a show with a panorama of vibrant blues, shot through with streaks of fuchsia and brilliant gold as the sun sank slowly into the cooling depths of the sea. A few scattered clouds served to diffuse the colors, making the scene look like an oil painting by Leonid Afremov. The warmth and beauty of that radiant orb in the sky brought me a moment of clarity; confirmation that there is definitely something greater than us out there.

Just then a short, plump older woman came in from the kitchen, and Elder Thomas introduced her as his wife, Rosey. Her broad smile and jolly disposition caused all of us to smile in return and feel at ease. I suddenly found myself enraptured by the delicious aroma of food preparation that followed her into the room. I was famished, and though I tried, I was unable to recall when I'd eaten last.

I momentarily forgot the delicious odors as I noticed Zoe and Ollin out on the paint chipped balcony. She had assumed a defiant stance as he appeared to be trying to engage her in meaningful dialogue.

I had just decided to join the duo on the balcony when I noticed Alasdair scrutinizing me carefully. He didn't bother to try and hide his disdain for me, and for some reason, that thought didn't sit well in the pit of my stomach. I shrugged and tried to convince myself his approval was not needed nor wanted.

"Keep watch Viv, we may be on sacred grounds, but we're much too close to the water, and I don't trust the tribal protection from that direction," Zoe confided to me.

"She doesn't even know how to use her powers properly yet, and you're telling her to keep watch?" quipped Ollin. "What is she supposed to do, ward off the malevolent forces by glowing?" He laughed hysterically.

His belittlement brought forth in me an inner desire to strike back. I raised my right hand which had suddenly turned into a dangerous heat source, though I was unsure of how it manifested. A surge of adrenaline excited my senses.

At that instant, something about me had changed.

For Ollin and Zoe as well.

A small funnel-shaped body of wind emerged in front of me, causing me to back up a little, but Zoe reacted even more quickly to Ollin's energy as she produced a water globe in the palm of her hand and lobbed it at his little tornado. Then she caused the wet little tornado to freeze solid, drop to the ground and shatter in tiny ice crystals. Not even faintly impressed with the effort he laughed maniacally, shifting the shape of his cloud into that of a serpent. I gasped recalling the dark dragon, chasing us on the freeway; it had been him all along.

In an effort to distance myself from Ollin's foolishness I descended the stairway into the backyard. I hadn't noticed previously that the back of the house was two stories. *I hope Ollin doesn't knock Zoe down these steps*, I thought to myself.

Zoe was relentless, dropping the temperature around her, she expelled her breath creating a protective crystal shield for herself. It was completely transparent, but there was a liquid fluidity to it, almost invisible but Ollin and I could see it, as his serpent coiled around itself but kept a safe distance.

I carefully stepped further back in the yard, in an attempt to better view the standoff between the two.

As one, they moved quickly to the edge of the deck, calling out in alarm which caused me to turn and see what had taken their attention.

At the far edge of the luscious green lawn, a distorted apparition sent an ear-piercing shriek through the air. The entity's pitch-black, long wavy hair, flowed down over what appeared from this distance to be a naked female body. Most of her was covered by her hair, including her face, but through it all, a pair of glowing red eyes stared out at us malevolently.

My knees buckled, and I fell to the ground, covering my ears with my hands as the shriek grew louder and more piercing. I curled into a fetal position, pressing my forehead to my knees. Images flashed in my tortured mind, of my dreams, of Tadeo.

That's when I started screaming uncontrollably as the sharp, cruel pain invaded every fiber of my being, and for the second time that day I blacked out.

* * *

A barely audible yet soothing beat penetrated my entire body, as I strained to identify the rhythm, I could make out the soft chanting of a tribal healing ceremony.

A shadow in the far corner of the room shifted as I quickly rose to my feet.

My voice was hoarse from the earlier screaming, "Show yourself!"

Alasdair moved into view, as my idiotic weakness for his piercing blue eyes betrayed me, sending flutters through my stomach and a flush of red across my face.

I growled deep in my throat, irritated with myself. How ludicrous to allow my stupid teenage hormones to dictate an infatuation for any member the opposite sex let alone this one.

Turning back, I noticed the bed that had probably been my refuge for who knew how long during my last blackout session. I sat down on it wondering who'd brought me here, to this room.

"You know, it wouldn't hurt if you showed those around you a bit less hostility," He said calmly as he walked toward the only window in the room, peeking through the blind.

His smooth voice carried an air of sophistication and a European accent that I couldn't quite pinpoint.

"Maybe if complete strangers would stop interfering with me and showing no regard for my feelings, I'd be more welcoming." I snapped back unkindly.

"Fair enough," he said, as he gently offered me his hand. "My lady, would you care to join our small assembly to discuss our peace agreement?" His voice carried a playful lilt, sending a flood of warm eagerness through me, so intense that I took his hand much too quickly.

Our touch created a spark that ignited a deep dark ferocity in me. Alasdair studied me with a startled look in his eyes. I quickly realized something radical was happening to him as well. He dropped my hand as if it had burned him and stepped back, combing his fingers through his dark, tousled locks. Still stunned, he met my eyes. We held each other's gaze for a moment, then he excused himself awkwardly. "The others are waiting for us in the dining room," and he fled without another word.

I was still a bit shocked and totally disoriented from the events of the day. Agitated and confused I went into the bathroom and reached above the toilet to unlatch the small window to let in fresh air. Pulling a clean hand towel from a stack on a corner shelf, I turned on the cold water tap at the antique pedestal sink. I sat on the rim of the clawfoot tub as I splashed my face with icy water.

The stinging cold numbed my face, as I turned off the water, blindly reaching for the towel.

An unknown terror rose within me as those same sinister red eyes stared at me from the mirror above the sink. Quickly I turned to discover no one behind me. I might have dismissed it as my imagination, except I detected a zephyr of air flowing out through the window, causing an eerie ripple in the curtain.

My hand trembled as I pushed open the door and half staggered out into the hallway. I was panting heavily and using the wall for support.

My knees gave out, and I fell trembling onto the hardwood floor.

An indescribable feeling came over me then; a need to pray. Already kneeling, my prayer was fervent as I pled for truth and knowledge. I didn't know what to believe anymore.

As I rose once more to my feet, slightly more composed, I turned and collided with my father. His worried face searched my own. He opened his mouth yet no words came out. I embraced him, feeling a deep need for consolation.

My usually strong father was speechless. *Maybe he feels as broken as I do*, I thought

He stroked my long chestnut brown hair pulled my chin up and kissed my forehead. I simply held on to him tightly, and he offered me a gentle smile.

"I wish this could be different, but it isn't. However, I'm beginning to suspect you are much stronger than I thought. The Calpulli will provide the necessary protection to see all of you through your training. I know it's a lot to absorb, Viviana, but I'm here for you."

Once again, many questions leaped into my mind at this most vulnerable moment. I pushed them back down. I trusted my father, but at that moment all I wanted was to move as far away from the bathroom and what I had just seen as I could.

We joined the others in the dining room. Not even the wonderful cooking smells could push back my fear as I looked out the window. I caught Zoe following my stare. Those red eyes were impressed on my mind, even when they were no longer visible.

Finally, I met Zoe's eyes, wondering if she too felt how insane all this was. We completely ignored Ollin's attempts to join in on our moment, as we smiled grimly at one another.

Throughout the dinner, Elder Thomas, Mr. Anderson, Humberto, and my father went over the details of Zoe, Ollin's, and my protection. They discussed how the Lummi Reservation was on sacred ground, which would effectively prevent the evil ones from crossing onto the land. I found myself unable to share my experience in the bathroom because part of me wasn't entirely convinced I hadn't manifested it out of my fear, so I just sat and listened.

"Why weren't Alasdair and I able to enter the reservation when we first arrived?" Ollin wanted to know.

Elder Thomas explained, "Certain individuals with special powers are forbidden entry unless they have a sacred invitation. You must all understand that the beaches themselves are not always safe. The salt water cleanses the land it touches. But power is just power, it's the intentions of the one using that power that matters. The intentions of the individual can infuse the powers with either good or evil."

"The eagle notified the tribe of your arrival, so a musical flute song was played to invoke the lighting of the path to you both, granting you permission to enter onto our sacred grounds." Elder Thomas continued.

I was about to ask him why I was allowed in when Humberto shared the story of the time when Zoe and I were first brought to the reservation as infants.

"The Calpulli knew of your arrival, as the divine prophecy patterns were evident." He said. Neither Zoe nor I pressed for more information.

We finished dinner and moved back into the living room. A knock at the door interrupted the conversation, and Elder Thomas excused himself to answer it. The others continued to strategize our next moves. Safety seemed to be their primary concern.

Shortly Elder Thomas returned with a young man of about our age, introducing him as Kenji, the grandson of one of the other Elders.

Apparently, we were all heading back to the beach for another gathering. I wasn't paying attention to the conversation as I absent-mindedly followed everyone outside. I was happy to learn that I was riding with Zoe once again.

The convoy was pretty much the same as last time, except Kenji and Elder Thomas rode with my dad and Mr. Anderson. My thoughts returned to Jim, our driver. He must have known more about all this than I did. I made a mental note to probe him later, as I stared at the dimly lit road ahead.

It was dark now, except for headlights and taillights, the only other light coming from the few houses along the way and the rapidly dimming night sky.

I opened the window to smell the ocean air. It was a familiar scent that brought back so many happy memories. As I took in the view, I started recognizing the area.

"This ceremony will be a reenactment of the tribal legend of the moon, the origin of Mount Si and the Forests," Zoe was saying. "This myth as it relates to the moon is somehow tied into our objective, the prophecy. All tribes have their beliefs and legends, but why this particular tribe's beliefs are somehow related to us, I don't know. I doubt anything of significance will be revealed tonight, as we are not yet complete," she trailed off deep in thought, then added, "Listen, what I'm trying to say is just allow yourself to be 'in the moment'. Nothing I don't already know is going to be revealed to Ollin and you tonight, so I can answer your questions later. But, it's not the only thing they will be doing. They will be casting a sacred invocation of protection over us so we'll be able to leave the reservation safely, and that's what I want you to focus on," she said, as she pulled off the road and parked the car.

CHAPTER SEVEN

I remained silent as the second-hand smoke from the pipe being passed around assailed my nostrils. Once again, a euphoric feeling wove its way through every fiber of my being. I was filled with a growing desire to abandon all my childlike innocence. A low moan escaped me as I opened my eyes, searching the faces around me. Almost everyone was staring straight into the fire and chanting. Ollin's eyes were closed, his body rigid. His jawline suggested an inner fortitude I hadn't noticed before. I tried to release the tension that was building in my neck, rolling my head back and forth, while slipping in and out of a dreamlike state.

I forced myself to avoid Alasdair's ice blue eyes which seemed to be staring right through me. My heart pounded as I caught myself wishing I was nearer to him. His eyes taunted me and a playful smile formed on his lips, sending a riptide of excitement through my veins.

Suddenly feeling embarrassed I sat up straight. I felt as if my mind was being probed. Trying hard not to look at him, I summoned a protective shield around me, and his eyes widened in surprise. He quickly looked away in an attempt to hide whatever it was he had felt just then.

I noticed Elder Thomas quietly studying the two of us. His face gave no indication what he might be thinking, though.

When the ceremony was over Ollin, and I stood quietly by the cars as the others talked, thanking the tribal Elders as everyone said their farewells. Zoe exchanged some words with Humberto and then leaned awkwardly towards her father for a hug.

My uncle Humberto informed us of the travel arrangements. Ollin was to ride with Zoe and me in the Audi; my Dad and Mr. Anderson were to take Zoe's car, and Humberto himself would go with Alasdair in the McLaren.

Zoe announced she'd drive since my nerves were still rattled and I readily agreed.

Just before we got into the cars, my father approached me, "Viviana, I know you must have a lot of questions, my sweet girl. I assure you I'll answer them as best I can, very soon. For now, you three get to the safety of the Anderson house, and we'll meet you there as soon as we can." He wrapped me in his arms, pressing his warm, loving lips to my forehead. His strength was very reassuring.

Zoe floored the gas pedal, revving the engine of the Audi before pulling out on the road. The car handled the curves of the road effortlessly, as we remained silent for a few minutes, putting distance between us and the others before any of us spoke.

"Don't take this the wrong way ladies, I just had you two pictured differently. You're not quite as fearsome as I'd envisioned," Ollin said, laughing softly as he sat back and rammed his knees into the back of my seat.

Ollin's comments put me on edge, "Do you mind taking your knees out of my back? Don't you ever think of anyone but yourself?"

I tried to control my anger, but a million questions were crowding back into my mind.

"Zoe, I've been extremely patient this entire day. I think it's time I got some answers." I was more perplexed than I'd realized. I cleared my throat and lowered my voice hoping to sound more in control. I reminded myself that Ollin was just over my shoulder.

Ollin leaned in once again looking back and forth between Zoe and me.

"Wait, what exactly do you mean when you say you want answers?" He sounded a bit panicked. "Please tell me you didn't just find out about the prophecy, today? Oh God, please say you've known about your powers longer than that!"

Zoe gave him a fierce look, before looking back at the road and swerving onto the freeway onramp. It was pitch dark now, and the only lights were in the buildings of the small towns that lay ahead. There was no traffic, and the sky remained overcast, with barely a sliver of moon peeking through. A sudden shiver passed over me, as I remembered the prophecy.

"Ollin, I only learned about the prophecy today. And I hate to break it to you, the same goes for my powers. Which to be honest, I'm still wondering if they're real or not." I quickly looked away, still seriously considering this might all be a dream.

The white McLaren crept up on Zoe's left, and Humberto motioned through the window for Zoe to lower hers.

"Turn on your phones!" He yelled through the opening.

Alasdair had looked straight at me before my uncle closed the window, causing another shockwave to pass through me, but I quickly looked away knowing I couldn't afford to have my emotions control me now.

Zoe asked Ollin to pass over her bag, and he tossed her a glossy black box-like purse. I immediately recognized the metal clasp logo from the Victoria Beckham line.

"Our phones are in there. I turned them off when we were at school," Zoe said. I reached into the suede lined purse and pulled out the phones before returning the purse to Ollin.

Quite a few text messages filled my screen, along

with seven voicemails, as soon as I turned my phone on. Most of the messages were from classmates. Except for one from my cousin Brian. I'd forgotten we had made plans for this evening. I replied to him, apologizing and letting him know I'd catch up soon. He immediately replied telling me it was all right, but he wasn't letting me off the hook that easy. I smiled as I texted back, [I'll call you this weekend. Promise.]

Being an only child had many disadvantages, but my cousin Brian was like a brother to me.

Caught up in my thoughts, I hadn't noticed when Zoe dialed Humberto. Their conversation was brief and somewhat one-sided as Zoe more or less just listened.

"What was that all about?" I inquired, as I purposely ignored Ollin and his attempts to encroach upon my space.

"They're headed to an emergency council meeting of the Calpulli. It sounds like they probably won't be at my house until sunrise," she said, without breaking her concentration on the road.

"OK, so are you going to tell me what's going on? Because what you just said has no meaning to me at the moment."

I wondered if anyone else had even bothered to consider how I might be feeling. Everything about this day had just been more and more confusing, and scary. Not to mention I felt like my imagination was running away with me at times.

"I'm truly sorry, Viv. And I know that doesn't

begin to fix the confusion of your day." She smiled. "It's actually quite normal that you'd feel this way, no one blames you." She took a deep breath as she changed lanes to pass a minivan with British Columbia license plates, a reminder of how close to the Canadian border we lived.

"I've told you about the prophecy, and the Elemental Linx. I knew the Council had already recognized the air elemental, but I had no idea it was Ollin. Like you, I only met him today. You both needed to be cleansed and protected with the Lummi Tribes sacred healing and protection. Only, today was intended for Ollin," she paused, "Viv, you coming into your powers, forced a slight change in plans. For the record, I didn't know today had been set aside for Ollin. They don't include me in these conversations." She said, sounding a little hurt.

"The Elemental Linx will fight the Moon God and his devotees. His disciples are not just gods of the underworld, but also deadly parasitic humans who've voluntarily committed themselves to serve the tyrants, in return for special favors of course. We have roughly twenty-four months from now to fulfill the prophecy. Should we fail the world will end as we know it." She stared off into the distance.

I slowly processed this new information. My dad would have a lot of explaining to do, to help fill in the blanks.

"We still have training ahead of us." Ollin looked pointedly at me. "Some of us more than others," he said proudly as he apparently thought himself much better prepared than I was.

"Yes, yes there will be plenty of training. And Ollin, I'm sure you'll be very pleased with yourself. But that's not what worries me right now. The fourth Linx has yet to be identified. Alasdair and Humberto seem to have a few leads, but no one can be certain until the fourth is with us. You see Viv until we are all together, we will not be able to come fully into our powers. Who knows what we can truly accomplish as a unit? The Elemental Linx must become linked so our powers can be magnified and our connection to each other, solidified. Otherwise, all the training in the world will be useless as far as our special powers are concerned."

As Zoe finished, I realized these bits of information were starting to make a little more sense. I also noticed the lights of the city coming into view and realized we were getting closer to our destination.

We passed the sign announcing the exits for the city of Everett and Seattle.

Two lanes opened out to five, and Zoe hastily moved into the left express lane. Traffic was getting heavier as I checked my watch. Only eleven twenty-six p.m. It felt much later than that.

"So Ollin, you now know a little about us. Tell us about you?" I said, unsure if it was him or his brother I wanted to know more about.

"What do you want to know?" He asked, with a smirk on his face.

"Everything."

"Everything? WOW, well, I suppose my life hasn't been much different than the two of yours. I attended boarding schools and got private tutoring. I've always had my brother to keep me company. He helped me a lot when I came into my element."

I shifted in my seat to get a better look at him.

"Your brother?" I inquired.

"Yes, my brother. You know, Alasdair?" he said. "Anyhow, our mom wasn't in the picture. We only ever had our father. He was a great dad. I often think how hard it must have been for him to raise us on his own, especially since we're so close in age; only ten and half months apart." He smiled to himself as if at a pleasant memory.

"Our dad was awesome. He explained to us all about our elements early on."

Zoe immediately interjected.

"Wait, what do you mean by 'our'? Are you saying Alasdair is an elemental as well?"

My memory yanked me back to the bedroom at Elder Thomas's home when we'd touched. Something had happened, and I thought I'd scared him; that I'd caused it. Now I wondered if he had been trying to conceal his powers.

"Yes, I'm saying both Alasdair, and I are elementals. But Alasdair's powers are not as strong since he is only a Guide," Ollin said as he looked at both of us, expecting us to know what that meant. "You do know about Guides, don't you?"

Zoe and I looked to each other, and while I

believed it was safe to admit I knew nothing, Zoe seemed to be a bit more reticent. The harsh reality that her father had kept more information from her than she'd thought was creating unresolved feelings. The sudden realization that Ollin just might know more than she did, didn't sit well with her at all.

Ollin proceeded to explain about Guides and their roles.

"Guides are elementally gifted humans, not as strong as the Linx but strong nonetheless. They are tasked with protecting the Linx from birth until either of our deaths. They are the ones who will train us, counsel us, and guide us through this calling." He said. "There are others with elemental gifts, but they're not as strong as Guides. A few serve in the Calpulli, while others live their lives as normally as possible, wanting no part in manifesting their elemental gifts." Zoe and I remained silent as he continued. "Then, there are those who want more power. They often become a problem to the Calpulli but are usually held in check. However, a few have moved to follow the darker forces, with the desire to enhance their powers," he trailed off.

I guess good and evil is in all of us. Some are given a special gift, yet the need for even more power overshadows everything, creating a never-ending lust for greatness, at any cost, I thought to myself.

"I'm pretty fortunate to have both my father and brother as Guides. Although I must confess, I have yet to master my element enough to overpower Alasdair." He smiled.

"So, what are your father's and Alasdair's elements?" Zoe asked.

"My father's is air, just like me. Alasdair's is much different. I don't quite understand it. It's almost like fire, but strangely different."

"Ollin, do you have any idea who our Guides are?" I questioned, looking him straight in the eyes, to ensure he didn't try to conceal anything from us.

He squirmed in his seat, uncomfortably.

"Listen, Ladies, if you two... well at least you Zoe don't already know, I'm sure there is a good reason. I'm not sure if I should be divulging that information."

"Damn it Ollin! If we're supposed to work together, live together, and protect each other's butts to see this mission through, we need to start trusting each other. Otherwise, we'll be putting ourselves at risk. So, you can start by telling us who our Guides are." Zoe's voice crackled with emotion, and a sudden chill followed her outburst. I reached within for my element, becoming more familiar with this tactic, to warm myself up.

"This is exactly what I was talking about, not being what I'd imagined." Ollin heaved a sigh. "Fine, you want to know who your Guides are, I'll tell you. Your fathers. It's not rocket science. Both of you should have figured that out as soon as I mentioned a Guides role." Letting out a long breath and puffing out his cheeks in exasperation, he looked out his side window.

The rest of the drive as we approached Seattle was quiet. I took in the familiarity of the scenery. We slowed down for construction and sped up as we moved through the downtown tunnels. Zoe signaled to turn off on Interstate Ninety. I realized I'd never been to her home. I didn't even know where she lived.

Her need for speed subsided as she drove through the Interstate Ninety portal tunnel and onto the floating bridge. As we took the first exit onto Mercer Island, I caught sight of the shimmering waters of Lake Washington.

Zoe pulled up to a monitored gate at the end of a cul-de-sac which opened to let us in as soon as she entered a code on the keypad. The entire area was meticulously landscaped. The house came into view with its semi-circular driveway, and Zoe pulled the car under the covered portico at the front entrance.

The house was an elegant stone and stucco mansion, sort of a hacienda meets villa style.

I had to catch my breath as we walked past the sitting room with its massive fireplace, big enough to swallow the three of us, without anyone noticing. The home's interior colors were warm and neutral.

We walked past the dining area right into the rec room. Zoe opened the expansive glass folding doors which lead to an outdoor living area, a swimming pool, and a gorgeous view of Lake Washington.

The infinity pool had a fountain spouting water up and over the side of the pool, like a rainbow. Everything was artfully lit, and I watched as Zoe flipped a switch to light up the outdoor fireplace.

Ollin rummaged in a refrigerator behind the bar

and surfaced with some bottles of water. I reached for one, suddenly realizing how parched I was.

I turned back and took a seat on the stone steps. Our six thousand square foot Georgian style home, while certainly breathtaking with its view of the lake from Capitol Hill, was not nearly as grand as this estate, nor was the view this serene.

Ollin took a seat next to me, interrupting my reverie. He didn't say anything, but his presence was enough to put me on edge.

"All this space back here and you have to come and sit right next to me? Was the car ride not enough for you?" I asked. I realized I had been too quick to flare up at him, and took a few deep breaths to try and calm myself.

"What is it with you two? I mean come on, give me a break. I'm trying hard here to keep my cool and be a gentleman, but you and Zoe's attitudes are making it very difficult."

I stiffened at his accusation. I guess he was trying, but I was still upset over the awkward introduction via the road rage. However, the three of us would be spending a lot of time together, so the least I could do was try.

"I'm sorry. Obviously, I've been a bit suspicious of you." I conceded.

He let out a 'ya think' under his breath thinking I wouldn't hear him.

"Your initial approach towards us wasn't all that friendly, you know." I jokingly reminded him. "But

I'm willing to leave that in the past," I said as I extended my hand. "I'm Viviana Magnus, pleased to meet you."

Ollin took my hand eagerly and stood chivalrously before me.

"My Lady Viviana, I am Ollin Seton." Kissing the back of my hand, he gallantly bowed before me. I couldn't contain my giggles, as I remembered his brother's formalities. I stood and curtsied.

ROSE CASTRO

CHAPTER EIGHT

I found Zoe sitting on a long sofa in the rec room, staring into the fireplace as if she was in a trance. She had wrapped herself in a brown plush throw. Her eyes were doing that obsidian thing again, and her face was drained of all color.

I could see Ollin was about to say something, but I tugged at his arm to make him stop. He looked around at me in confusion, but I had already turned my focus back to Zoe. *I wonder what's going through her mind right now?* I thought.

She stayed like that for what seemed an eternity but in reality, was only twenty minutes. Ollin had taken a seat outside in front of the fireplace, so I leaned through the doorway and focused on the fire in front of him. I experimented, using my thoughts to make the flames dance and change colors. Ollin caught on to what I was doing right away and used his air element to try and disrupt my focus. He flashed me a taunting smile, as we both fought to maintain our composure.

Turning back to the rec room, I nearly jumped out of my skin, startled to find Zoe standing over me.

"Do you feel it?" she whispered softly to me.

Ollin and I looked at each other, unsure what she was talking about.

Before either of us could say anything, Zoe shushed us and said, "Let your elements guide you."

She sat down next to Ollin, reaching for our hands, as I moved to join them. We listened to her instruction, "Quiet your minds and flow with your elements."

I noticed Ollin was keenly focused, but I was still confused. I had no idea what flowing with my element meant.

I sat there staring into the flames of the outdoor fire.

A pitch-black sky with a blood red moon. It seemed illogical. There was a faint rustling off in the distance, but I was unable to see anything, only marvel at the unbelievable darkness around us. I reached for the familiar warmth of my element within me, as I conjured a beacon of light from my element and aimed it out into the darkness. A vision of strange winged creatures appeared, their voices echoed in our heads, via telepathy, speaking as one. Their faces were angelic, but their bodies appeared as ethereal as mist. I could just make out that each creature had six wings.

"Please do not fear us. We are the Seraphim. We can only appear to you in a dream state so we must be quick. The Calpulli will guide you, train you, and die for you. There is much to learn. Legions are working against you and the others, but in due time you will be shown who the real enemy is. For now, know that the prophetic Elemental Linx is in harm's way. Your greater purpose is to save humanity. It is imperative for the survival of the human race that the Five Pendants of Creation be restored to the temple of your ancestors before the fourth blood moon. Go now, take the others and flee from this place. Find a safe haven until the Guides return. Hurry, or you will run out of time."

"What on earth?" Ollin rushed to grab me as I started to fall forward.

I looked at them both, a bit dazed.

"Viv, what just happened?" Zoe was still speaking in hushed tones. "Your pupils were dilated and your face as white as a sheet. It was a bit scary."

As Ollin held me to keep me from falling, I stared again into the fire.

"Didn't you see them? Hear them? The Seraphim gave me a warning. We need to leave here right this minute. We're in grave danger." My voice choked a little as I tried to hold back tears.

Zoe and Ollin made eye contact and nodded, deciding not to argue with me.

Grabbing her phone Zoe pressed one number, then spoke in such muffled tones that I couldn't make out what she was saying, or perhaps I simply blocked out the conversation.

Ollin moved to close the glass paneled doors, but Zoe hollered at him to leave them as the three of us rushed through the house to the front door. Zoe yelled for me to start the car as Ollin and I rushed out to the driveway.

Zoe followed us out not even bothering to close the front door behind her. She jumped into the front passenger seat and yelled: "Go, go!" I stepped on the pedal, peeling out of the portico and up the driveway. The main gate opened slowly as I aimed straight for it.

"Head for the freeway, Viv. Where are we supposed to go anyway?" she asked looking over her shoulder.

"I have no clue, I'm not from around here," Ollin muttered.

"What did they tell you, Viv? Did they give any instructions other than just leave?" She pressured me.

I headed up the eastbound ramp for the freeway, as I told them of my vision. They both listened attentively, saying nothing until I'd finished.

"I don't know where to go." I blinked back the tears.

But then as I looked at the freeway signs, I spotted one for a familiar exit. "I know where we can go," I said, as I stomped my foot down on the gas pedal and we sped off into the night.

Brian, Chad, and Lindsay are my cousins on father's side of the family. Dad's sister Aunt Maggie married a self-made millionaire who developed a software company a few years back and sold it. Then he repeated the process, landing an even bigger sale. These days he consults with various software developers and on some secret government contracts. But he mostly just enjoys being a family man.

While they could easily live on a huge spread, they opted for a more traditional home in a lodge-like setting in Ravensdale. The fifty-acre property is home to horses, cattle, alpaca, and their many dogs.

My uncle believes in earning your own way through life, so his lifestyle involves raising kids the 'good old-fashioned way.' We all know what a softy he is when it comes to his family, though.

Cousin Brian lives in the pool house and is completely self-sufficient. The only times he needs to venture into the main house is for mandatory family dinners, game nights, or movie nights. Even though he's a high school senior, and continues to play club soccer, he works part time for his dad, helping in whatever projects he can. "Zoe dial a number for me on your phone, will you?" and I reeled off Brian's number from memory. She dialed then handed the phone to me.

"Hello," I recognized Brian's voice immediately.

"Hi, Brian. Would you mind some company for a day or two? I've got a couple of friends with me. I hope that's all right."

"Sure, I'd be happy to see you again, and your friends are more than welcome. How soon will you be here?"

* * *

Driving the back-country roads reminded me of when my mom and I used to drive out for visits. Mom was a rancher's daughter, so she loved spending time on my aunt and uncle's property, so much so, she'd convinced my dad to invest in property not too far away, where we kept horses. She'd escape at every opportunity to come out and ride, and when we could, we'd come as a family and spend time there together.

When we arrived at Brian's, the security gate was already open just as Brian had promised. I drove slowly through and veered off to the right on a small private driveway towards the pool house. Brian was waiting outside.

Even from a distance, I could tell Brian's face was a bit pale. I was sure he'd perceived the urgency in my voice, especially when I asked him not to tell anyone.

Brian towered over me, but he still managed to bend down and give me one of my favorite hugs.

"What on earth is going on Viv?" He asked.

I cleared my throat to introduce him to Zoe and Ollin, and then we followed him into his bachelor's pad. His eighteen hundred square foot living space was fabulously decorated.

"Sorry, Brian," I said, looking to Zoe and Ollin, hoping one of them would jump in as we hadn't even thought to collaborate on a story. I tossed the car keys and my phone on the coffee table.

Ollin shrugged his shoulders and looked at me

sympathetically, whereas Zoe avoided any eye contact altogether. I was on my own.

I'd never kept secrets from my cousin. He'd stood by me all this time, as he helped me get through my mom's passing. We'd had a standing Friday night date for the past few months, and while I thought we'd missed today, it turned out I was right here, probably where I needed to be anyway.

"Something came up…it um…well, I can't go into specifics at the moment. Trust me, I wish I could Brian, but…" *Oh, how am I going to explain what was happening?* I wanted to tell him, but I couldn't, at least not until I could better understand what was going on myself.

Zoe and Ollin had found their way to the soft leather sectional. But thankfully Zoe realized I needed help, so she moved to join Brian and me.

"Thank you so much for allowing us to stay here Brian. We definitely appreciate it." She hesitated for a split second and continued. "Our dads are away for the weekend. They're all good friends. We were going to crash at my place, but, well to be perfectly honest with you, we creeped ourselves out."

We all waited for some reaction from Brian, but he only gazed at Zoe, waiting for her to finish.

She looked down for a moment, and I could have sworn she was blushing. But just as quickly as the color appeared in her cheeks, it was gone again.

"We attended a rather strange pow wow earlier this evening, and I think we're still a little shaken. I'm sure it's nothing, but Viv suggested we should come here, and we agreed."

Ollin looked annoyed as he jumped into the conversation.

"Just to clarify, it was their idea, and there's no winning with these two," he said as he scowled at Zoe.

A small moment of satisfaction overcame me. Ollin had probably felt his ego a little threatened by Zoe's story. My little smile of triumph quickly disappeared when Brian looked directly at me.

"I want the truth, Vi. I've known you all my life. Heck, I know you better than I know my own sister, so I know when you're withholding information from me or lying; and to be perfectly honest with you, I get the impression you're doing both. What kind of trouble are the three of you caught up in? You look neither tweaked nor drunk, so what is it?" He stood there, arms crossed.

Yes, of course, he would suspect something, and Zoe's story just served to fuel his suspicions.

"So, what is it? Because I'm not buying the story about a pow wow."

I tried to respond, but I had nothing, and he was right, I didn't know how to lie to him. He was one of the few people who could see right through me.

Just as tears started forming in my eyes, Zoe's cell phone rang. We all turned to her, I with a sense of relief at the opportunity to collect my thoughts.

Zoe turned as if to walk away, but I gave her a nasty glare that held her to the spot. But as I thought about it more I could understand her need for confidentiality and recognized it wasn't fair of me to keep her there where she couldn't speak freely. So, in all of our best interests, I directed her towards one of the bedrooms and closed the door behind her.

The interruption at least kept me from crying and gave me a bit of strength back to try to convince my cousin that our imagination simply had gotten a bit out of hand. Not once did Ollin try to interject. He only sat there staring, looking upset. I was pretty sure Brian didn't believe me, but he didn't press the issue. He only stood, towering over my five foot four, with his six foot one looking dubious.

I excused myself to the bathroom so I could splash water on my face. Once there I looked around cautiously remembering my last incident in a bathroom, as a chill ran through me. I took a bath towel from the pewter towel hanger and tossed it over the mirror, making sure to tuck it in on all sides. I had no desire to see mine or anyone else's reflection tonight; imagined or otherwise.

When I returned, Zoe was sitting thoughtfully in the same spot as before. Ollin was in the kitchen with Brian getting drinks, and from the smell of it, making popcorn, as the buttery aroma penetrated my nostrils. My stomach growled at me, reminding me I hadn't had an actual meal all day. The dinner was delicious, but I had been too rattled to eat much.

I sat down next to Zoe, breaking her meditative state.

"Is everything alright?" I inquired.

"Yes, as far as the Calpulli are concerned. I told them we'd decided to crash at your cousins. I believe they all felt it was a good idea, but they didn't quite understand what prompted us to move in this direction. I didn't say anything to them about your vision. Or what Ollin or I felt for that matter," she sighed.

I'd been so caught up in my vision, I hadn't thought to ask what they'd experienced.

"What exactly did you feel, Zoe?" I looked at her more seriously.

Zoe looked over to where the guys were chatting and looked back at me.

"I'm not exactly sure. Ollin came into his element before any of us; just a few months before me. We obviously were both very young. But I knew from your father and Humberto that he'd felt something when I first used my element. I never knew what it was until you first used your element. It was like a tug the first time since you didn't necessarily come into your element right away. But today you did, and I felt a terrific jolt internally. My insides were burning. Ollin felt the same. So, when you were out of it, Humberto explained to us that we were creating a connection; a bond so to speak to your fire element. This evening at my house it would appear we may have been making a connection to the earth element, as I at least felt my innards rumble, like an earthquake. But there was something strange happening. I can't explain it, as it was accompanied by a sudden wave of fear." She whispered as she finished.

Once again, she stared blankly into space as if trying to search internally for that feeling once again.

Brian and Ollin rejoined us with a bowl of popcorn and some hot cocoa. Ollin had no problem making himself at home as he deposited himself right beside Zoe in a casual manner; stuffing his face with a fistful of popcorn.

My cousin sat down next to me and handed me a cup as he noticed Zoe's absent expression. He leaned in as I was taking the cup from him, "Is she OK?" I simply looked at him gratefully and nodded.

The next hour was spent in casual conversation. Ollin and Brian bonded over soccer, bantering over the U.S. National team. Zoe pretty much kept quiet, only answering questions directed at her and smiling politely. In the end, we were all exhausted and needed desperately to get some rest.

Brian showed Zoe and me to the guest room and set up a make-shift bed on the sectional for Ollin.

As we settled in for the night, Zoe and I agreed that Ollin needed to be included in any conversations involving any new developments; it was only fair. Exhaustion contributed immensely to our agreement, and in no time at all, we were both asleep.

CHAPTER NINE

The sun beamed down on us as we made our way toward the natural wooded area I'd seen the previous night. A warrior about my age walked beside me, and I wouldn't have thought anything of it, but he was eyeing my cleavage. I was now dressed in a similar loin cloth to the others, except mine had a cleverly built in skirt of sorts. The high strapped sandals were more comfortable, and the top much better fitting, although a bit more revealing, hence the attention from my walking partner.

I was intrigued by the hammered gold bands on my left arm. One just above my wrist and another much more detailed, encircled my bicep. They reminded me of the bracelet I had admired at Tiffany's only a week ago. My skin bore a painted design resembling jaguar spots. On my head was a massive headpiece which I could only assume was that of a jaguar as well. The fact that I was looking out through an open mouth with huge curved teeth was a big clue. I could see feathers of gold and jade hanging from the headpiece. Similar feathers hung from the top straps of my sandals and my arm cuffs as well.

In my left hand, I carried a shield bearing tribal markings, and in my right, I held a spear. The obsidian tip looked deadly, and the long carved wooden shaft fit comfortably in my hand.

We walked together in unison, and as I looked ahead, the Warriors I could see were bald, except for a single long braid over their left ears. Their heads were painted, one-half blue and the other half either red or yellow. I chanced a glance behind me and noticed most the Warriors were in similar vestments to my own, representing either eagles or jaguar. Their regalia, however, was much more resplendent than mine.

My walking partner looked back over his shoulder, to see what I was looking at. When everything appeared to be to his satisfaction, he merely grunted and pressed onward. A small triumphant smile came upon me. *Made ya look.* I taunted in my mind.

As we advanced deeper into the thick forest, I noticed the ground was rising and I realized we were at the foot of a volcano. A sudden eerie recognition crept over me. I knew from my geography classes we were in a lush basin, surrounded by mountains and many volcanoes.

The headpiece weighed heavily on my shoulders, as I surveyed the surrounding area. The Warriors ahead now changed formation, moving to left and right, merging into a single line. My partner walked forward to the center, so I followed him as the warriors that flanked us took their places slightly behind us. I realized there weren't as many warriors as I'd initially thought.

We stood there peering through a dense fog. It was then that I noticed Tadeo was also at my side. Like me, he wore vestment's resembling a jaguar. His scalp, was half blue and half red, with a thin braid of hair hanging below his chin. *I don't remember seeing that before.*

I felt a little disappointed when he didn't even bother to look at me. I wasn't sure if I should say something, but at that moment my thoughts were cut short.

Two females emerged from the fog. A sudden urge to run came over me. I started to call forth my element, as those dreaded red eyes stared straight at me once again, mocking me.

The woman with the red eyes was deadly gorgeous. She wore an ornate brassiere, with crescent moons holding up her breasts, and small round suns rising above them. The two halves were held together in the middle by what was obviously a full moon. The entire garment was fashioned of black leather, trimmed in dark red. Her abs were perfectly defined, all the way into the low-cut leather shorts that hugged her slim hips and thighs. Her long black hair was secured in a braid which hung over her shoulder. Long black leather boots completed her ensemble.

Her companion was of similar build, sporting the same long boots and short hip hugging shorts, but she wore a corseted top that covered more of her midsection. Her platinum blonde hair flowed straight past her shoulders, and her eyes were an unbelievable shade of violet.

Tadeo stepped up next to me as if to protect me. I couldn't help wondering what would happen next. *What's going to happen now?* I wondered.

It was then I noticed the heat in my fingertips. Unsure at that moment exactly what was about to happen, I knew I would at least try to do something should the need arise.

Zoe had told me their names, but all I could remember were her nicknames for them. Micteca the goddess of the underworld and Coyolxa the moon goddess. *The trouble is I don't know which one is which*, I thought to myself.

"Mictecacihuatl and Coyolxauhqui, you are far from your dominions. What brings you here? We have no quarrel with either of you." Tadeo wasn't asking, it was more of a statement.

I stood there taking in the menacing looks of the red-eyed beauty. I now realized why it had been so easy for me to mistake her for being naked before when her hair was covering her.

She studied me carefully. Her obvious challenge strengthened my resolve not to quiver. I knew the flame in my own hazel eyes was visible as I'd called upon my element.

"Tehuatl!" The violet eyed girl said to Tadeo, to which he merely smiled. "Mixpehpena. It has been foretold." She announced emphatically.

Her irritation with Tadeo piqued my interest. I would have to inquire about that later, adding it to my list of many questions.

"Mictecacihuatl, I'm not happy to see you either. Trust me. Mixpehpena, yes indeed, I am the chosen one." *Not like I had a choice*, I heard him say under his breath.

So, the blonde one was Micteca, and the fierce one Coyolxa, who was now laughing derisively.

"Well, well. The two of you have a history. Oh, please do tell. Not all of us get to enjoy the spoils of earth," she said snidely, pacing back and forth.

Oddly, neither of the goddesses nor Tadeo could cross the invisible threshold between them.

Through the dense fog, came the sound of growling and scuffling. Squinting hard I thought I could make out glowing orbs; eyes perhaps?

Looking over my shoulder, I felt reassured by the warriors gathered behind us.

"Nonsense, we are here for that one, Tadeo." The jut of her chin indicated me. "Hand her over and avert a full-scale attack on the human race that your gods love so zealously, yet leave unprotected." Micteca let out a throaty laugh, which startled me. Maybe it wasn't the laugh, but the fact that she was asking him to hand me over.

My element was radiating from me now, as I heard several gasps from behind. I turned to see that a few of the warriors from the back row had stepped out of formation to enable them to see me better, as the front line remained steadfast. Their reaction helped to bolster my confidence.

Coyolxa stood on the other side of the invisible line, arms crossed in a defiant glare, but Micteca took a few steps backward, arms at her side in an attitude of combat readiness.

I'd completely forgotten about my shield and spear, suddenly realizing they were engulfed in flames.

Tadeo looked at me and in his eyes, I could see my reflection, my flames dancing in his vision. After a few seconds, I felt a calming come over me, and I called my element back.

"Interesting." Was all that Coyolxa said as she turned, ready to walk off into the fog.

"Tadeo, you know you cannot protect her where she'll need it most, where she belongs, in her own time. We give you until the first Blood Moon to hand her over. Otherwise, you've been warned. You know what your resistance will cost, and you know how to find me." Micteca gave me a scornful look as she walked away, taking the fog with her.

The forest cleared, and the sun peeked through once more.

Tadeo gave some orders in Nahuatl and grabbed my arm, yanking me with him as he strode purposefully ahead of the Warriors. I tried to pull my arm loose from his grip.

"What on earth is wrong with you, you're hurting me!" I shrieked.

He loosened his grip but didn't let go. As a matter of fact, he walked faster, and I practically had to run to keep up.

I looked back briefly to see that the rest of the warriors were headed in a different direction. I wasn't sure if I should be particularly scared at that moment but instead of demanding answers I kept pace with him as best as I could.

Finally, we reached a river and followed along it's bank to a place where it disappeared into the mountainside. Tadeo finally released his grip on me as we slipped inside a cave entrance. I stood still at one side for a moment as I waited for my eyes to adjust to the dimness. Gradually I could make out the dark waters of the river as it flowed out of sight into the depths of the cave.

Tadeo had disappeared briefly from view, and I was startled to hear his voice close by me as he spoke loudly enough to be heard over the splashing of the river.

"Let's go."

He had pulled a canoe from concealment behind some rocks and set it in the water, holding it against the shore by a short rope. He held an oar in the other hand and motioned for me to get in. I very much wanted to object but decided it would save time to just do as he asked.

The canoe didn't seem very stable as he paddled in silence, barely making any a sound as the oar entered the water and Tadeo propelled us forward with a smooth, steady motion.

As my eyes adjusted to the ever-changing light, I could see places where water dripped down the cave walls. The river was narrowing and the noise level rising accordingly. As the water started to move faster, I held on tightly to the makeshift seat, not knowing what to expect.

The serenity of a few moments ago was gone. In its place, the thunderous rumbling was getting louder as the wood canoe began to pitch wildly on the turbulent water. My adrenaline level rose sharply. There was no need to call my element this time as it rose protectively on its own, protectively, causing the water in the bottom of our small vessel to steam. My knuckles went white as I tightened my grip on the sides, and my breathing became labored. I'm sure I screamed more than once or twice, but the roaring water drowned out the sound. The final stretch of rapids dropped us some fifteen feet, as Tadeo somehow maneuvered us safely through with me hanging on for dear life.

We now found ourselves in a large placid pool. I tried to see how deep it was but could make out only blackness below us.

I finally exhaled in relief as Tadeo steered us toward another narrower tunnel on the far side of the pool. As we entered the tunnel I could see a bright light ahead, so incandescent as to be almost blinding after the darkness we'd just come through. The small tunnel widened abruptly, and I gasped as we emerged into a breathtakingly beautiful underground temple.

Tadeo vaulted from the canoe, pulling it up on the white sand shore of the underground chamber, and offered me his hand. I took it gratefully, fearing my nerves and legs would betray me, but I said nothing, noticing the water had washed away his warrior paint, so I assumed mine was gone as well.

Brilliant crystals lining the walls of this cave, were the obvious source of the incandescent light, as well as support for the lush vegetation which grew in abundance; many exotic flowers I didn't recognize, and I'm not sure why I was disappointed when I didn't know what they were.

Warriors dressed only in loincloth and capes, bald except for a simple braid, wearing sandals, and each holding a weapon, were stationed at the bottom of the temple steps. They didn't speak, but acknowledged Tadeo with a nod, ignoring me completely.

We climbed a small flight of steps and were greeted by two warriors who exchanged a few words with Tadeo, as he instructed me to remove my headpiece. It was only then I remembered with surprise I still had it on. He removed the cape he'd been wearing which was drenched and handed a smaller one to me. I turned away to make the change and noted my lack of a bra. I allowed a moment for the red in my face to simmer, hoping no one had noticed.

I pretended to be interested in the architectural details around the entrance as Tadeo concluded his dealings with the two men.

Finally, he nudged my elbow, "Time to go," he said. I nodded for him to lead the way and we set off.

We walked along a tall narrow corridor, lit by torches and more crystals. Hieroglyphics on the walls were interesting but meant little to me, as I couldn't decipher them. The corridor soon opened into a large bright hall with many ornate carvings.

Directly ahead of us were four grand thrones, and as we approached them, I could see the light reflecting off shallow pools puddles of water which lay within a depression carved in the floor. The design depicted a huge compass which appeared to light up as Tadeo and I passed over it, but it could have been just a trick of the light.

It was obvious the thrones were empty. They were clustered around a solid crystal pillar, so tall I couldn't see the top of it and wider than my outstretched arms could reach. As we got closer, I could see there was an alcove cut into one side of the pillar in which lay a huge obviously ancient book. I stared open mouthed as hieroglyphic letters appeared in the air above the book, etched in pure light as if by magic.

As I stepped closer to get a better look, the cover of the book slammed shut, and the letters vanished, causing me to stagger back in surprise.

Then right before my astonished eyes, the thrones

were suddenly occupied by four stern-looking men of advanced age.

One by one they each spoke.

"I am Xipe Totec, God of the Seasons, death and rebirth of nature, nurturer to mankind. I control the gods of the north," said the man furthest to my right, with dark hair, pale skin, and very dark eyes. He wore a light blue cape that glistened and a loin cloth like the rest.

"I am Tezcatlipoca, God of Temptation, punishing mankind for evil and rewarding goodness. I control the gods of the west," said the man furthest to my left. He had dark hair as well, with a bit more color to his skin, and ice blue eyes. His cape was bright crimson.

"I am Quetzalcoatl, God of Civilization, representing forces of good and light pitted against evil and darkness. I control the gods of the east," said the man left of center, with blond hair, vibrant blue eyes, and tanned skin. His cape was as white as the driven snow.

"I am Huitzilopochtli, God of War, the eagle, the Turquoise Prince. I control the gods of the south," The man who was to the right of center had deep chestnut hair, hazel eyes with a touch of gold and olive skin. He wore a turquoise cape.

These gods were nothing like I'd seen depicted in statues. Somewhat surprised I took in their features, wondering if my astonishment was noticeable to them. These had to be the Four Aztec Gods of the creation story Zoe had shared with me.

"Please let us know when you are finished gawking so we may proceed with this assemblage. I prefer to spend as little time on earth as possible." The man furthest to my left, Tezca... oh, I wasn't going to remember the name. I now fully understood why Zoe had come up with the nicknames. Tezca it was.

I felt myself blush at his comment when I suddenly remembered my top was still wet, and nervously tugged my cape closer around me. I attempted to call forth my element, but it wouldn't come. I was struck by confusion. *Why won't it come?* I tried again.

"Don't bother summoning your element. Your power is neutralized in our presence. We learned long ago that our creations could and will become our worst enemies. We give you the powers, and we take them away at our discretion." Quetzal said, with a warm smile. "I know some of my brothers are eager to return to their mundane existence, so we will make this as educational as possible. We understand the Water Linx has explained the prophecy to you already?" I nodded in agreement, so he continued. "Good, that will make this little meeting go much quicker." He stood up then, towering above me at what I could only guess to be seven or eight feet. I only know he was very tall and had a physique that made the Greek gods look like weaklings. In fact, these gods all had similar physiques.

He walked slowly around the perimeter of the compass on the floor with his hands behind his back.

"You see Viviana, our Father created us in his image, with very similar abilities to his, albeit not as powerful. We, in turn, did the same with our creations. The world… well the world got somewhat out of control with the beasts of our creations, and we sadly had to destroy it and them, more than once, unfortunately. We eventually diminished the powers of our creations, significantly, and very few would learn to tap into their 'gifts' so to speak. The Calpulli are an example of this. We made it so because, while we cannot reveal our true nature to the average man, we still need him to do our bidding. Unfortunately, we are unable to cast all our current ruinous creations from the earth, for that would require us to destroy earth once again." He then returned to his throne.

"What my brother is trying to warn you against, are the treacherous beings you and your fellow Linx will soon encounter. Danger will come to each of you in many forms, always tempting you and using your weaknesses against you. It is important that you follow the Calpulli's instructions to the letter. Train hard, learn much, and most importantly find the fourth elemental so that the Linx will be complete. Only then will each of you reach your true status as gods and goddesses of the new era." Xipe Totec's voice was much more kindly, but like the others, it still carried an air of superiority.

"I have a few questions. If I may be so bold?" I cleared my throat, attempting to sound more confident than I felt. "Who and where is the fourth elemental? Are you delivering this same message to each of us, or just me? And why here, like this? You are extremely powerful beings. Why not back home, in my time? I mean it didn't stop that maniac goddess from showing up practically on my doorstep."

Tezca looked as though he was about to summon lightning and send me straight to hell, but Huitzi stood and walked towards the pillar before us.

He held his hand above the book. It flew open, and the pages flipped in a sudden flurry, stopping just before the end. Once again, strange words appeared in the air, as he stared down studying them for a moment. He finally looked up, as the book closed more softly this time, and the floating words vanished.

Huitzi looked at Tadeo, and they stared at one another in solemn silence. I looked back and forth at each of the gods and Tadeo. No one seemed to remember I was even there, as they remained in a meditative trance.

"It's so like you men to exclude a lady from your discussion. Gods or not, it's very rude." Emerging from a side passageway, a beautiful dark-skinned woman appeared. Her hair as black as ebony, and eyes the color of jade. She stopped right beside me, and I caught a whiff of floral fragrance that enveloped her. I noticed a small nosegay of tiny five petal flowers carefully tucked behind her right ear. Their centers were deep orange, the petals mostly bright yellow fading to white at the edges. Her skirt was styled similar to mine. However, hers matched her brilliant jade eyes, and her top was much more revealing than my own. She wore a similar ornate shoulder piece to that of the four brother gods, which held her gold cape in place.

"I am Nahui Atl, also called the Lady of the Jade Skirts, and I was the fourth sun until these men decided it was a privilege I shouldn't be entitled to. They destroyed my island of Atlan, and along with it, my people." She glanced sideways at the gods. "We were a peaceful, advanced civilization. But in their jealous hatred, they flooded the earth. Because I am the goddess of water, I was not destroyed, a minor detail they overlooked when they cast me from the sky. So instead of killing me, they kept me as one of the last gods to roam the earth and do their bidding." *A very informative greeting*, I thought. Wishing everyone could take a page from her book.

Nahui Atl walked towards Huitzi, saying something in a native tongue. He turned his attention to me.

"The one who protects the Codices, the ancient texts of our people, which are mostly proof of our existence, of our creation," Nahui Atl said as she circled him, staring up at the other three gods one by one, finally resting her gaze on me, once again. "They were having a telepathic conversation when I arrived. They forget their manners, as it's not often they find themselves in the company of a young elemental, a future goddess." She winked at me as she turned to Tadeo mumbling something under her breath which it seemed neither he nor I, understood.

"There is much to be learned, Viviana. You had questions as I walked in and interrupted, so, allow me to answer them for you." She stood beside me again, facing the brothers.

"The gods cannot intervene in the prophecy. They can provide various methods of support to you and the others, but they cannot do anything that will directly change the course of events. Because of that, they cannot tell you where the earth elemental is or who it is. You are the only one of the Linx with whom they will communicate directly, and the only one who will travel to our ancient grounds and times," she said, looking at the Four Gods again. "Your fire element is stronger than the rest, perhaps not yet but it will be, and the fire element is the only element that will be able to get close enough to the sun when the time comes. Which brings us to your final question. Why meet here and not in your own time? Though you have a guide in your time, Tadeo here is also your guide. He is tasked with training you in ancient combat methods against the vengeful gods and their wicked combatants. He will also be a liaison between you and the higher gods."

Huitzi gave her a withering glare as she slowly took a seat on the steps to one side of Xipe Totec, avoiding any further eye contact with the other two.

"Yes, now that you've had your answers, allow me to add the final words of this encounter. As the God of War, I expect you to train hard in both realms. I have no tolerance for laziness, nor do I accept any excuses, not even death. If I must breathe life back into you to see this prophecy favorably completed, I will." Huitzi said, with intense force. "Is that understood?" The roar was so loud the entire hall echoed, vibrating the crystals as if he'd intended to make music.

"Yes," I whispered.

The Four Gods stood tyrannically over us, as Nahui Atl remained seated.

Just as they had appeared, they abruptly disappeared.

I collapsed on the floor, bewildered and in tears. Tadeo attempted to assist me back to my feet, but Nahui Atl pushed him off. They exchanged words, but I was too upset to care.

She comforted me as we sat, allowing me to cry into her jade skirt. Her hands gently caressing my hair, soothing me.

I was a little ashamed of my outburst, but a good cry seemed to be exactly what I needed.

CHAPTER TEN

When the tears finally subsided, I raised my head to scan the great hall. Nahui noticed my searching look and gently shook her head. Tadeo wasn't there, and I was disappointed.

My cheeks were flushed from sobbing as I scrambled to my feet, ashamed of myself. I'd allowed the gods to scare me. Some warrior I'd be for Tadeo.

"You don't have to be strong, at least not immediately, especially not under these unusual circumstances."

I looked at Nahui, realizing she was the only one to see me for what I was, a frightened seventeen-year-old girl from another time. She brushed back my hair with her hand, as I deeply inhaled her calming scent.

"Why are you helping me?" My voice squeaked slightly, and I trembled a little, fighting to keep myself from calling upon my element. Her gaze remained focused on my face, and her jade eyes were reassuring.

"Because it's my job to keep you and the others safe, at least as safe as possible. I'm not allowed to fight your battles, but I am authorized to travel with you and share any direct knowledge I've acquired of your enemy, so you may use it to defeat them."

"What did you just say?" I asked, making a desperate attempt to control my emotions.

"You heard me. I exist now, and in your time, I'm immortal. I do the bidding of the higher gods, which isn't much, so I spend my time in deep slumber when I'm not roaming the earth, helping the Calpulli. I will reappear to you and the other Linx to assist in the capacity I've already explained. But for now, you need to focus, and just know I will come to you again soon." She caressed my cheek with the back of her hand once more before she walked away.

I made a weak attempt to call her back, but she quickly disappeared through the portal through which she'd entered. Letting out a deep sigh, I pulled my hair over my shoulder. A habit I'd inherited from my mom when she was pensive.

"What are you thinking about?"

Tadeo's voice startled me as I quickly released the handful of hair I'd been toying with, trying to look strong, but instinctively I shrank back awkwardly.

What the hell was *is* wrong with me, now *isn't* the

time to be a coward. The heat rose within me, and I allowed it to radiate from my skin as he stood there unfazed by my reaction.

Just then we were interrupted by a warrior at the entrance of the grand hall who cleared his throat to gain our attention. Tadeo broke his gaze and looked around at him. The warrior said only two words in Nahuatl to which Tadeo simply nodded and once more we were alone.

I hadn't even noticed him move, but suddenly he was directly in front of me. "I'm truly sorry Viviana." His jaw muscles flexed, as he carefully took my face in both of his hands, crouching, so his face was in front of mine. "I wanted to explain everything, but it wasn't my place. Now you have a better understanding, especially of my *job*," emphasizing the last word as if it carried more meaning for him than for me.

"You clearly have your work cut out for you. Training me won't be an easy task. We should probably get started soon. I don't know how much longer I'll be here." I stepped back, putting distance between us. I knew I might have sounded a bit bossy, but I wanted to be straightforward and not linger in his touch. I couldn't allow myself to form any attachments, not when so much was at stake.

A tiny smile twitched on his lips, but he turned so quickly I didn't have time to think about it. "Follow me."

Our ascent up the inside of the mountain was treacherous. My limbs soon burned with fatigue, but thankfully we finally reached a small landing. My legs were so wobbly they could barely support me.

A cave opened off the landing and Tadeo motioned for me precede him inside. Two warriors were waiting there, but unlike the others, they seemed genuinely happy to see us, exchanging hugs and handshakes with Tadeo. This was a display of camaraderie I hadn't witnessed in this realm. Tadeo spoke less stiffly to these two, as they took turns staring at me. I didn't return the gesture, pretending to stare off into the cave and listen to the running water that echoed from somewhere beyond.

"So, you are Viviana, the fire elemental?" I turned, startled, that a warrior had spoken to me in plain English. I met Tadeo's eyes, and he smiled at me reassuringly.

"Yes," I replied, still unsure which one had asked the question.

As I carefully studied the two, I realized they were as young as Tadeo and I. *Just how early does the selection process for a warrior begin,* I wondered to myself.

Like Tadeo, but unlike the others, the of them were fair skinned with features that were more European. They each stood as tall as Tadeo, with long wavy locks. Their eyes were hazel like Tadeo's and mine, with hints of gold caused by the torches lighting the cavern, and reminiscent of Huitzi's.

I must have made them uneasy, as they both fidgeted, but one of them finally decided to introduce himself and his partner.

"I'm Elisha, and this is Vitale. We will be seeing you later during the hand to hand combat training."

The one named Vitale smiled warmly, but Tadeo was already leading me away. "Come, we must be going."

I wondered why Tadeo wouldn't allow me to converse with them longer, but my thoughts quickly dissolved as we proceeded down a steep and narrow pathway. The roar of tumbling water greeted us as we reached a river. I assumed it was the same river we had arrived on but I wasn't sure. I watched as Tadeo dragged out yet another canoe, almost identical the one in which we'd arrived.

"This will get us back into the city much quicker than walking," he said, gesturing for me to get in.

I reluctantly jumped in and braced myself for another rough ride.

Leaving the mountain wasn't nearly as traumatic as our entrance had been, except for the final drop. That was nearly enough to make my heart stop.

Our speed had increased as the noise level rose and suddenly we were ejected from the side of the mountain with such force that we were in freefall. The foaming water dropped out from beneath us, and for the next few seconds, we were in free fall. The canoe started to turn over in midair, and Tadeo hollered, "Jump!"

Thanks for the warning, I thought, but used my anger to propel myself clear of the canoe.

We plunged feet first into the water, and I

immediately started kicking my way back toward the surface. I'm not a very strong swimmer, but I broke clear and took a desperate gulp of air. However, my ordeal still wasn't over as I found myself floundering against a strong current. I had already swallowed more than one mouthful of water when I felt an arm encircle my waist and heard Tadeo's voice in my ear telling me to stop fighting, so I did. He pulled me towards calmer water and helped me back into the canoe which floated there calmly as if nothing unusual had happened.

As I bent over the side of the boat, coughing and spitting up water Tadeo thumped my back helpfully, then took his place to resume paddling as I tried to regain my composure, still coughing and gasping. I was exceedingly grateful for the rescue, and sat there wet and exhausted, reliving the past few minutes that I'd feared would be my last.

"We're getting close to the city. I don't think today is a good day to start training, do you? I glanced back over my shoulder at him.

My voice was hoarse from expelling water, "No, I'd appreciate a bit of rest. I know it probably won't please the gods, but I just don't have it in me to train just now."

As the city gradually came into view, everything around me slowly faded out of focus.

CHAPTER ELEVEN

When I rolled over in bed the next morning, the pain that radiated through my entire body was excruciating. Zoe was still sleeping, so I pulled myself up slowly, careful not to disturb her. With some difficulty, I made it down the hall and into the bathroom. I knew my cousin kept extra toothbrushes in a drawer, so I grabbed one and brushed away my morning breath. I splashed water on my face and after a glance in the mirror tried to tidy up my bed hair. Meanwhile, every inch of my body screamed at me to go slow.

Making my way toward the kitchen, I bumped into Brian. A muffled giggle escaped me. I was starting to feel a little more like my old goofy self. He smiled as he offered me his cup of coffee, but I declined.

"A painkiller is what I need right now. Do you have any? I was just on my way to hunt some down."

Turning with a quizzical look, he opened the door to the pantry and pulled out a first aid kit. He shook two pills from a bottle as I filled a small glass with water at the sink. Having swallowed the pills, I sat down at the kitchen island, glancing over at Ollin, who was apparently still in deep in slumber. Good, I wasn't ready for him to wake up just yet.

Brian stood across from me sipping his coffee and arched an eyebrow questioningly.

"So, are you going to tell me what's going on with the three of you?"

I'd been expecting this. Brian had always been very observant. We had always been close, but over the past few months, we'd grown even closer thanks to his helping me through the sad time after my mother's death. For that, I would always be grateful.

"I promise to share everything I can, Brian, but for now, I must ask you to trust me a little longer, at least until I've spoken to my father. I'm not at liberty to discuss any particulars yet." I reached for his free hand, relieved when he took mine in his and squeezed it as a sign of reassurance that he'd be there for me, no matter what.

"Viv, I trust you implicitly. Just remember, you're not alone. OK?" He shifted his gaze over my shoulder and stiffened visibly. I turned to see what had caught his attention. Zoe was standing there, arms wrapped around her midsection, looking every bit like she'd just rolled out of bed.

A small giggle escaped me as I grabbed her by the arm. "Come on, I'll show you where my cousin stashes the toiletries."

A flush of pink invaded Zoe's face, as she averted her gaze from Brian.

I closed the bathroom door behind us, and she looked in the mirror with astonishment.

"Good grief! How embarrassing that your cousin saw me at my morning worst." She fussed, as I tapped her hip to move over so I could find her a toothbrush.

"He doesn't care about those things. He's not shallow like that. Besides, why do you care what he thinks?" I handed her a new toothbrush.

"For your information, I do care about my appearance…I'm a little vain like that. As you must be as well since you look fairly presentable."

There was no denying it, she had me there.

Once I'd ensured that Zoe had everything she needed, I returned to the kitchen. A glance at the other side of the room confirmed that Ollin was still as dead to the world as he had been a few minutes earlier, even with the slight commotion, we'd created. I wondered if his deep sleeping would pose a problem, later, if we were ever in real danger again. From all indications, we were sure to be at some point.

Brian was on the phone. He gave me a broad smile as he pulled me in for a much-delayed hug. I wondered what had taken him so long, but brushed that thought away as I allowed myself to feel safe in my cousin's embrace, even if for only a moment. As he wrapped up his call, Zoe rejoined us, clearing her throat to make her presence known.

"So, what shall we do now? Have you heard from either of our fathers?" I asked her, as I stepped away from Brian and joining her by the kitchen island.

"No, I haven't. I already tried calling my dad, but he's not answering." She seemed to be commenting more to herself than to me.

"You're all welcome to hang out here as long as you need to. I don't have any major plans today…well, except for family brunch over at the main house." Brian and I chuckled as we both knew implicitly what that entailed.

"Oh, brunch with the family, how awful for you," I chided Brian. We had a history of kidding each other when we moaned about something related to family togetherness.

Brian grinned back at me, "Okay Smarty. I guess I can live through it if you can."

"I don't think we have much choice since we were told to stay here," Zoe said, fidgeting with her hair.

I finally realized her uneasiness was being caused by Brian who was carefully studying her every move. Then it hit me, Brian and Zoe might actually be attracted to one another. I guess that wasn't so surprising, especially since they were both very attractive people. Zoe typically had an aura about her that would send guys and girls running in the opposite direction. However, she seemed quite smitten with Brian. Well, in a Zoe kind of way. I smiled to myself at the thought.

In an attempt at discretion, I made my way towards the sitting room to give them a little privacy, easing myself down on the end of the sectional which wasn't occupied by Ollin.

As I went through my phone, I discovered a few text messages, so I responded to them briefly: *long story, nothing earth shattering, catch up at school, family weekend.* Although it didn't begin to cover the entire truth, it at least bought me time to pacify my friends.

A message from a number I didn't recognize popped up on my screen. Good morning. Your dad's phone died, so we will use my phone until further notice. I'm glad you're at Brian's, please stay put till we arrive later this morning. Your uncle Derek knows you're all there, so he's expecting all of us for brunch. It was signed Uncle Humberto.

Zoe seemed to be getting along well with Brian, so I took advantage of the moment to do some research in my browser. I typed in Aztec legends, skimming through the results, nothing stuck out. So, I cleared the search and typed in four blood moons. A few interesting articles based on theories, but nothing remotely close to what I was looking for. Then I typed Aztec legends of four blood moons. Again, nothing. Aztec prophecies produced nothing that seemed to be tied to what I'd heard over the past day.

Ollin shifted positions in his sleep, reminding me of how we'd just met, which also reminded me of the

Lummi Reservation and the previous day's events. I typed in Lummi prophecies and legends. But still, nothing of any significance came up.

I sat pensively trying to form a correlation between the Lummi tribe and the Aztecs. Both had myths or legends centered around the sun and the moon which I found quite interesting. I'd have to give it more thought later, as Ollin's eyes were now open and staring right at me.

"You know what? You're a very heavy sleeper?" I countered his glare, commanding the upper hand, at least for the moment.

"Good morning to you too." He said as he got up to tidy his space. He seemed a little grumpy. Maybe he wasn't a morning person, or maybe he felt like crap the way I did when I first awoke, and the way Zoe had looked.

I decided to take it easy on him and explained where everything was so he could clean up. He thanked me politely and disappeared down the hall.

I gathered the spare blankets and pillows and returned them to the linen closet. Ollin was on his phone in the hallway. Unsure why I was eavesdropping, I did so anyway.

"I don't know what's going on, but it was crazy...I was afraid. For the first time, I was genuinely afraid." He grunted, taking what seemed to be a calculated deep breath. I took a hesitant step back, but then Ollin's voice grew more impatient, so once again I got closer so I could listen.

"Alasdair, whatever is going on, whatever you know, don't keep me in the dark." He broke off into a different language, so I took it as my cue to walk away before he caught me eavesdropping.

It seemed Ollin was just as puzzled as Zoe and I. Somehow this set my mind at ease, knowing he wasn't keeping anything from us.

Back in the kitchen, Zoe and Brian were much more relaxed with one another, and as much as I wanted that trend to continue, I had to update Zoe, so I broke into their conversation.

"Excuse us for a few minutes, Brian. We have a little something to discuss." He was refilling his coffee cup, so I added, "Would you mind pouring one for Ollin too? He'll be out shortly."

R. CASTRO

CHAPTER TWELVE

After the introductions to Brian's family, we all slipped into a comfortable rhythm. Humberto phoned to tell us to start brunch without them. Teasingly he said, "We certainly don't want to be held responsible for any starving teenagers."

I checked to make sure Ollin and Zoe were not feeling out of place. I recognized they may be missing their own families, and I knew that any connections we could make with one another, would help to ease the absence of our own family members.

Brian and Eric did an excellent job of making Ollin feel right at home as they discussed soccer, while Lindsay chatted Zoe into complete boredom about cheerleading. I took some satisfaction in all of us being seated comfortably around the breakfast bar, at least until Aunt Clarisse took the seat next to me.

"You OK sweetie? You know I'm not trying to pry, but you look… well, you look awful." She smiled, and I noticed how the imprint of time showed on her forehead. Aunt Clarisse was known for her bluntness, and I loved it. Something she and my mom had in common.

"I'm fine. Some days are harder than others, but I think I'm making progress, you know?" I said, smiling into her beautiful green eyes, a Magnus family trait. She was the female version of my father. Like he, she too was a bit more rustic in comparison to the other Magnus family members, who were posher, more prim and proper.

As she gently gripped my hand offering reassurance, we both understood that no further words were needed. It was a nice feeling, even if I wasn't ready to fully open up to her, as I could with Brian, at least I knew the option was there.

Just then the gate monitor announced the arrival of a vehicle. Ollin, Zoe, and I tensed up a bit, unsure what the arrival of my father and the others would bring. I slowly discarded my unfinished food in the bin, placed my dish in the dishwasher, and made my way to the family room, where everyone else was gathering.

I purposely avoided eye contact with Ollin and Zoe, as I could sense their unsettled emotions conflicting with my own. From the corner of my eye, I noticed Zoe looking my way. Finally, she got up and discarded the food from her plate when she realized her efforts were not working to get me to look at her. Ollin, on the other hand, seemed oblivious and continued to work his way through yet another plate of food.

We'd anticipated our father's arrival so much, but now I felt the need to avoid them a bit longer. I turned swiftly on my heels and fled toward the bathroom. My stomach was tied in knots as I made my way towards the only available safe space, then realized that Zoe was right behind me.

"Wait, Viv!" There was a nervous tone in her voice as she grabbed at my arm. I turned and waited, knowing she probably still didn't know her way around.

"What?" I said a little too harshly.

"Where are you going?" She asked uneasily. Both of our emotions were high, causing our elements to form stronger connections.

"To the bathroom. I just need a moment to gather my thoughts and bolster my courage, I guess." My voice faltered as my eyes welled up with tears.

The overwhelming emotions were so strong I didn't bother to hold back the tears rolling down my face, as I rushed toward the bathroom with Zoe in tow.

She stood quietly waiting for me to compose myself, as I splashed cold water on my face, wondering if anything unusual would happen this time, as it had at Elder Thomas's house. Zoe's look was telling me I needed to pull myself together.

"We have to get back out there. Our fathers are

probably already here, wondering where we've disappeared to. Besides, I don't want Ollin left on his own with them." Understanding her meaning, I followed her out of the bathroom, but not before taking another quick glance at myself in the mirror.

My father eagerly pulled me to one side as soon as we appeared, to inform me that he and I would be heading to our ranch after, which wasn't too far away.

"You don't have to take this in all at once, Sweetie. I know it's a lot, but I'm here for you. We all are." I could hear the caring in his voice as he pulled me to him for a reassuring embrace. I didn't reciprocate, I was still ticked about his hiding stuff from me.

I certainly wasn't prepared to be going to the ranch. After all, I hadn't been there since Mom passed away. I knew Dad escaped there on occasion to go horseback riding, and the property was preserved as if she were still with us. That's what he wanted, for her memory to live on at the ranch, her personal eternal sanctuary.

CHAPTER THIRTEEN

Majestic evergreens stood solemnly peering down at us, as we drove the back country. Deftly maneuvering the soft curves of the road, I gripped the steering wheel tightly. The sun had to work hard to penetrate the overgrowth of trees, but they shielded me from the reality I needed to ward off for a little while longer...*just this drive*...all I wanted was this drive and not to have to think about elements, prophecies, warriors, and death.

The familiar sights brought back distant memories as if understanding everything I'd been living through. The countryside felt alive as if calling to me, soothing me, easing my passage.

When we arrived at the ranch, the gate was open.

The others, of course, had opted for the shorter route and were there before us.

Bright colors adorned the paths, and fall foliage set the place ablaze. A view to be envied as always. That's the way she had planned it. The warmth of that memory brought a smile to my lips as I recalled the conversations she'd had with the landscapers. She wanted the property to always look vibrant, full of color and life. Not an easy feat in the rainy Pacific Northwest, but they had come through for her.

I glanced at my companions, Ollin and Zoe, as I steered towards an open parking space in the garage. Their faces bore supportive smiles, but their mood was somber, much like my own.

"We're here. So, what next?" I asked turning off the engine.

"I think we should allow the Calpulli to start the conversation. We'll hear them out, then we can ask them about anything that remains unclear." Ollin said.

Zoe and I agreed, so we all headed into the house breathing deeply of the invigorating mountain air as we approached the front door.

I fully expected Mom's boisterous laughter to fill the house the moment we walked in. But of course, that didn't happen. I was overcome by an involuntary shiver, but Zoe was once again at my side touching my arm. No words were necessary. A silent understanding existed between us. The courage she offered, helped me pass over the threshold, my heart racing as waves of panic cascaded over me.

I was suddenly unsure of my footing, my vision becoming blurry as tears flooded my eyes. Thankfully my companions acted quickly, and the two of them quietly whisked me into a small study off the main entrance.

Like a relentless dagger, the pain stabbed my heart repeatedly. Gasping sobs escaped my throat as Ollin closed the doors behind us and I sank into an armchair. His pale complexion and Zoe's serious expression belied the empathy they were feeling for me. It was comforting to know someone else understood what I was going through. Their eyes said it all…they understood.

"Whenever you're ready, we'll be right here at your side." Zoe's voice was full of compassion, an unusual trait for her, as she and Ollin embraced me.

The room was suddenly filled with a warm misty breeze. It was our elements coming together as one.

We finally understood. A moment of clarity overcame us all, as we stared into each other's eyes. There was no denying how changed we were. Our eyes easily betrayed us when our elements took over. Most people wouldn't understand. Differences are often feared or labeled. If the last twenty-four hours were even a tiny indication of our powers, caution and control would be the first things we'd have to master.

There we stood, the three of us destined to save humanity. The very same humanity who would most likely lock us up and experiment on us if they ever found us out. The gods in their twisted plots had selected us, the Elemental Linx, to stand up against Tecuciztecatl, the Moon God. The Tetrad Prophecy, our prophecy, the sole reason for our existence.

A deep feeling of resolve seized me as I jumped to my feet. Our destiny had become my reality, and I was ready to own it. Swallowing all lingering fear and doubt, I opened the French doors into the foyer, "Let's do this, Linx," I winked at my companions as they both followed me out.

As we arrived in the family room, our elements once again joined forces as if in solidarity. Alasdair was the first to notice our entrance, but Humberto was the first on his feet, in a curiously defensive stance.

The tense facial expressions of those in the room gradually relaxed as if by a concerted effort. *Did we startle them?*

Just as I was pondering that question, a familiar scent assailed my nostrils. At that moment, I caught a movement in my peripheral vision to my right. Turning, I confronted an unexpected guest. A woman who'd only recently entered my life, Nahui Atl, Lady of the Jade Skirts sat there as large as life and twice as bold.

The brilliance of her smile reminded me of my mother. Brief melancholy passed through me something like a shimmery thread reaching out from her toward me. I would have brushed this off only days ago, attributing it to lighting or something else more logical. But today I knew better. I could feel her energy the same as when she'd soothed me before, so I was familiar with it.

As I was about to speak, my father stepped into view.

"There you are," he said smiling at me and gathering me to him for a reassuring hug. His arms felt safe. Many questions immediately rushed into my mind, but I could feel Ollin's energy prodding me as a reminder of the agreement we'd made earlier, to listen to the Calpulli and wait before we pressed for further information.

I squeezed my father back warmly this time, "in the flesh," I said jokingly.

With a hand on each side of my head, his eyes sought mine as he teared up. "I'm so sorry for all of this mess, Sweetie. I should have told you much sooner, but I could never find the right moment... and well, life had other plans. It just seemed like too much of a burden to add to everything you were going through." He inhaled deeply.

A calmness enfolded me. I knew it was Nahui Atl.

"Dad, it's OK. I mean we can't go back and change what's already been done, but you have to trust that I can handle anything you tell me going forward. I may need a moment here and there, but we can't go on keeping information from each other." I thought back to my dream experiences. Tadeo...the gods...and her.

R. CASTRO

CHAPTER FOURTEEN

The group proceeded to recap everything we already knew. Zoe's patience was waning rapidly, and Ollin and I kept giving her sideways glances hoping she'd remember our agreement, to wait for the Calpulli to finish before we jumped in with our questions. I sincerely hoped they'd soon offer up some information we didn't already know.

Considering all I'd been through, I realized I must have been in shock earlier, but I didn't press for more information. I was kind of irritated with myself the more I thought about it.

I felt Nahui Atl again reaching out to me telepathically. Her face bore an empathetic expression that reminded me of her warm embrace. I compared the feeling to my yearning for my mother.

Nahui Atl spoke up, "Please excuse the interruption, but I haven't been properly introduced to these young people." She boldly made eye contact with each of us.

"My most humble apologies," Humberto apologized profusely, as he moved to stand beside her.

"This is Citlalli. She's the highest-ranking female in the Calpulli. We joke that she keeps the rest of us in check, but her primary objective is to provide the Linx with weapons training," he said as he regarded her respectfully. "She specializes in the art of Aztec weaponry." He smiled at her then turned to the rest of us, "You will each select a weapon, which you'll learn to use in combat." He went back to his seat.

As if on cue Mr. Anderson disappeared into the library, which struck me as a bit odd. He seemed familiar with the layout of the house.

"Thank you, Humberto, for the introduction. I'll most likely address you as Linx most of the time, and only by your individual names when I'm referring to you directly." Citlalli's voice was smooth, yet commanding as she took the center of the room, we all gave her our undivided attention. I wasn't sure if she was using some kind of emotional manipulation, but even Alasdair regarded her respectfully.

At that moment, Mr. Anderson returned carrying a long, bulky leather bundle which he placed on the large table in the center of the room. Citlalli walked gracefully to the table, making me acutely aware of her captivating figure. She looked pointedly at Zoe, then Ollin and finally rested her eyes on me. I could feel her gaze penetrating my core, attempting to stir my element, as I fought her for control. I realized she was only toying with me, as she could no doubt override my powers at a mere whim.

Untying the strip of leather which bound the bundle, she ever so subtly cleared her throat.

"These are the weapons from which you will choose, and the one remaining will go to the Earth Linx."

The others shifted restlessly. I wondered if the slight change in their demeanor was caused by the prospect of choosing our weapons or the mention of the fourth Linx.

Once opened, the bundle revealed some powerful lethal looking weaponry.

"These weapons have been enhanced from their original versions. But before I explain each one, I want the three of you to gather around, and allow the energy of the weapons to speak to your soul. You will know instinctively which weapon is yours." Though she was very serious, she looked excited at the same time.

Zoe and I stood on one side of the table, while Ollin approached from the opposite side.

She wasn't kidding. I didn't even take notice the other instruments as I reached for a deadly looking long spear-like object. The blade was a cross between a Samurai sword and a machete, though much more elegant. The metal, while shiny was a bit darker. The long handle was dark black and looked heavy, but the entire weapon was surprisingly light. It just felt so right in my hands. I looked to see what Zoe and Ollin had chosen, or maybe I should say what had chosen them.

Zoe was holding a pair of twin blades. The blades were black, while the handles were highly polished wood.

Ollin's weapon was rather unusual. Just a simple length of rope with a leather pouch at one end, along with a satchel. I couldn't make out exactly what it was.

The last weapon on the table was some sort of odd looking boomerang. The tips were rounded, and they were formed entirely of metal similar to my weapon's blade.

I backed away from the table to gain enough room to deploy my weapon to its full extension.

"Interesting that the *tematlatl* would call to you, Ollin." Citlalli circled the table to him. Gently placing a hand on his shoulder, she reached for the rope contraption.

"Why do you say that?" his voice was raspy.

"It's actually a simple sling with a few improvements of course. The ancient warriors used stones, but this one comes with obsidian darts, infused with poison." Looking back at the table, she stared at the lone object laying there.

"That is the *cuauhololli*. It was originally designed to be thrown at running targets. The rounded part on the end, the club, would bowl the target over. This enhanced design does that as well, but then it returns to its handler, like a boomerang," Quickly Citlalli switched her focus back to Ollin, "Both weapons do the most damage after being launched in the air. I was curious which one would be yours. After all, you are the Air Linx."

Facing Zoe, she chuckled. "I'm not surprised by your choice of the obsidian blades. Your weapon, except for the handles and the finish of the blades, is the only one that has not changed from the original. The blades are cut from obsidian stone, then polished and fitted with Snakewood handles."

Zoe looked more closely at her weapons. The blades, eerily beautiful, gave off an energy of their own and were well matched to her small build.

I rested the shaft of my spear on the ground, facing Citlalli as she approached.

"Yes, of course, the tepoztopilli. The fire element would hold the most impressive of the weapons. It's impressive in that it makes the loudest statement."

I overheard a chuckle behind me, realizing it had come from Alasdair. Momentarily I wondered if he'd still be laughing if I was holding my spear to his neck.

'Your weapon has undergone the biggest transformation. While still operative as a spear, it also acts as a sword. It has the length and curvature of a Tamahangane sword, the width of a machete, and it's forged to perfection, with a light, yet strong carbon steel. The handle was originally made of oak, but yours is made of Quebracho, a Spanish wood."

Allowing my right hand to caress the girth of the

long handle, I appreciated the smoothness of its finish. Citlalli was right, it was certainly a most impressive weapon.

A sudden déjà vu came over me. At first, it was a hazy confusion, but as I allowed my subconscious to filter the memories through, I realized I'd seen these weapons before, in their original form. Tadeo and his warriors. I was overcome by a rush of energy as I welcomed the memory.

Unsure how long I'd been lost in thought, I caught Alasdair's quizzical stare. A blush once again betrayed me. I looked away to avoid his eyes, only to find Humberto equally fixated on me.

As I shifted my stance, I heard a small gasp from Zoe. Turning to face her I thought I detected a glint of fear in her eyes. Those dark eyes which had become even darker as I had noticed they always did when there was danger present. Ollin moved to her side protectively. I swung around, looking over my shoulder, convinced some malevolent being was in our company, only to be met with further alarm on the faces of the others, except Citlalli. She merely regarded me in with an amused expression.

My confusion led to panic, and I felt rattled and a bit faint-hearted. A tremor passed through me, and terror began to grow as everyone seemed to be pulling back, putting a safe distance between them and me.

Citlalli circled the newly created space the others had made, pulling her long hair into a knot.

My element was burning savagely from within. It

was only then that I noticed a stinging sensation. Flames rose from my skin emitting a translucent bluish glow. I struggled with a feeling of nausea in response to the heat within. It felt as if I was losing control.

As the heat penetrated through me, I gradually became more aware of my surroundings. A sea of blue flames cavorted, ceding to my thoughts. Recognizing the need to harness my element, I yielded to Citlalli as she sent a cooling mist in my direction. Part of me wanted to beg her to stop, but my conscious understood my element needed to be contained.

I'd reached a moment of complete awareness during the ascending experience, but now my thoughts became disorganized once again. The feeling of awareness gradually dissipated, to be replaced by hopeless despair as I collapsed to the ground.

Citlalli knelt beside me and serenely took me into her arms, just as she had in the underground temple.

Tranquility settled over me. I knew it was Citlalli. Gradually my breathing evened out, and I slowly composed myself.

My father approached cautiously. Falling to one knee, he reached out and stroked my head lovingly. Tears…tears just happened.

Uncontrollable tears made their way down my face, and onto Citlalli's shoulder. I held on tighter to her, as I breathed in her calming floral scent.

It was Zoe who approached next, breaking the silence to inquire if I was okay. I felt her concern on a deeper level and wished we were in private at that moment.

Citlalli slowly released me and took with her the warmth I had found so soothing. She looked approvingly at my father as he helped me to my feet.

I closed my eyes, searching for lingering traces of my element. My stomach betrayed me with a loud rumble.

My father chuckled, and I slowly became aware of those around me once more. I looked at Zoe, and as we gazed into each other's eyes, I hoped she would understand that I needed a few moments of privacy to pull myself back together, and soon.

I then faced Ollin who appeared to be extremely frustrated, pacing back and forth in front of the French doors. He seemed to have no interest in looking at me. Instead, he settled for the view outside.

I made a mental note to inquire of him later what was bothering him.

Humberto stood with a smile pasted on his face, but anyone could see it was for show, to create a sense of normalcy.

"Come, sit over here," my father requested as he led me to the sofa. The very same sofa currently being occupied by Alasdair. He was, however, focused on his brother, and only glanced briefly in my direction.

I broke the awkwardness in the room, looking for answers.

"What happened? To me I mean?" unsure whether I'd asked the question correctly. I cleared my throat, "Why did everyone move back?" That was what I really wanted to know. Their frightened looks had been very unsettling. I needed to understand what had set them off.

Clearing his throat, my father spoke. "Your element Viv. You need to understand we're not too familiar with a fire elemental, especially for a Linx." I could tell he was choosing his words carefully.

"What do you mean, you're not too familiar?" I pressed.

"Well, to begin with, fire elementals are rare. Very rare. And in our experience, those who've expressed such elements have been rather low-key, especially for a Linx. So, we're all learning right along with you about your element. We have writings about this of course, but no firsthand accounts, at least not like we have on the other elements." He continued trying to comfort me by stroking my arm.

Trying to fathom it all, I noticed Alasdair at Ollin's side. They weren't speaking to each other, but it was hard to miss the look of concern on Alasdair's face. Funny, I hadn't even noticed him leave the space he'd been occupying next to me, only moments ago.

Zoe broke through my thoughts, suggesting... no, demanding that she accompany me to the bathroom to splash cold water on my face. Thankful she'd finally picked up on my subliminal message, I took her hand, and we scurried away.

Just then a memory popped into my mind. When Alasdair and I had touched hands briefly, there had been a very strange discharge of energy between us.

Before disappearing down the hall, I looked over my shoulder, only to find Alasdair and Ollin were gone.

CHAPTER FIFTEEN

As we entered my bedroom, Zoe locked the door behind us. With one finger to her lips, she checked the bathroom, then the closet. When all was clear to her satisfaction, she grabbed me by the arm and pulled me into the closet. I flicked the light on as she secured the door, and laid a rolled-up towel across the gap at the bottom. I was fascinated with her desire for extreme privacy.

She walked to the back of the closet, put her back to the wall, then she slid down it until she was seated on the floor. I joined her.

"Are you OK?" She searched my face for clues to my condition and state of mind.

"Yes, I think so. I'm just... well to be perfectly

honest, I have no idea?" The feeling of uneasiness had never left me, but my need to get away from the others had most likely concealed it.

"You scared me. You scared everyone." She considered her last words then proceeded. "Well, maybe not Citlalli. She didn't seem afraid, or surprised." I sensed the latter was more of a question, something she was curious about.

"I truly have no idea what happened. You all were suddenly gasping at me, and not in a good way. Then everyone moved back." I struggled to control my breathing. I didn't want to get worked up and cause a repeat episode. Zoe stared at me intently, probably ready to react if necessary. But it wasn't necessary, I was all right.

Or at least I thought I was. Suddenly I felt lightheaded, dazed and confused. I tried to shake it off, but I must have passed out.

* * *

It was dark out, as I sat up and looked around. A few feet away I could make out the silhouettes of at least a dozen warriors. One of the men passed close by and grinned at me as if to acknowledge my presence.

The night was mild, but it was evident my wet clothes had dried on me. I combed my fingers through my tangled hair in a futile effort to improve my appearance. I was about to stand up when I noticed Tadeo, asleep nearby, sitting with his back against a large tree. Even at rest, he looked stoic and dangerous. My eyes lingered on him a moment longer. He was gorgeous, reminiscent of an era when teenage boys were brought up to be fine young men. There was something about him though that didn't fit in with the rest of the warriors. It wasn't just his fair skin and hazel eyes.

I don't know how long I studied his features, but when I finally shifted my gaze elsewhere, I spotted Vitale and Elisha from the mountain. Elisha was sleeping, Vitale eying me curiously.

When I made direct eye contact, he gestured for me to follow him, so I did.

As he led me away from the others, I found it difficult to keep up with his long strides, but as soon we were far enough away to talk privately, he halted and smiled.

"Are you all right?"

He too was handsome, but certainly not my type. He was more of the 'boy next door' type. Quite good looking, but very much aware of just how attractive he was. The conceit came across in his demeanor.

"I think so." I hesitated, noticing my voice was still raspy as it had been ever since Tadeo had saved me from drowning.

"Good." He looked toward Tadeo and Elisha, then back at me, speaking in a more hushed tone. "I'm not sure what you know, and I'm not at liberty to share much. But I will say this, you need to keep your head during the training. Stay focused," he looked past me again, taking a deep breath.

I could tell there was a lot more he wanted to say,

as he pushed his fingers through his wavy locks. Pacing, he muttered something under his breath, before looking back at me.

"Training is of the utmost importance. Without it, you will not survive, and we will continue to be stuck here..." He trailed off as if preventing himself from divulging too much information. "What I'm trying to say is don't get distracted." He looked very solemn.

We stood there, each thinking our own thoughts. It was obvious what, or should I say who the distraction was that he was referring to.

I forced myself to stand taller, adding a tinge of haughtiness to my voice.

"I can't think of anything that would distract me. I do know I'd prefer to be home, in my own place and time." I said, with a small, grim smile, my eyes not leaving his.

He acknowledged the challenge, returning my smile.

"I'm glad you understand. Why don't we get started on your hand to hand combat training? If you're up to it?" he teased.

I wasn't about to start making excuses. "I'm as ready as I'll ever be."

Vitale proceeded to explain the very complex martial art form known as Krav Maga, and how to use it in real life combat situations. He shared some history of how it was developed in Israel, and if used correctly it was the quickest possible way to defeat an opponent, by striking at their most vulnerable body parts.

I listened intently, wondering how he knew a relatively modern martial art. I made a mental note to ask him about that later.

As a footballer, I already understood offense and defense, so he dove right into explaining kicks, strikes, self-defense, escapes, ground fighting, etc. He outlined the various forms of weapons defense, emphasizing how going into combat unarmed against a weapon was dangerous. I had to roll my eyes at that, it seemed so obvious?

His voice faded as my thoughts wandered back to my own weapon, the tepoztopilli.

Shaking my head to clear my thoughts, I looked back towards the campsite where the other warriors still lay in slumber. I was determined to learn more about the Linx's weapons in their original forms. I didn't want my training here to be wasted. I needed to take this new skill set and knowledge back to my companions.

I interrupted Vitale, "Tell me about the weapons the warriors use. For instance, the tepoztopilli." I purposely inquired about my own weapon first, though of course, I didn't mention the reason for my interest.

He laughed, rather loudly for my taste.

"You've received your weapon already, have you?"

Unsure of what he knew, I was determined not to pry for information. That, I planned to leave for Tadeo.

"Please, just answer the question. We don't know how much time I have here, so the better informed I am, the better equipped I'll be to help you… us." I did my best to keep my tone friendly, though I wasn't entirely sure he was someone I wanted as a friend. An ally, perhaps, but a friend?

Taking a deep breath of the night air, I felt more determined than ever to make this work.

Vitale shrugged, "It's the standard front-line weapon of our military. But don't let that fool you. It is also the most difficult to master, which is why it's the first one we throw at the newest recruits. If they can handle the tepoztopilli, they can handle the others with ease. It's extremely useful in slashing, thrusting, and any form of hand to hand combat."

He sneaked a peek back at the others, taking a shallow breath.

"You need to get the lady Nahui to show you the Codices. Typically, they're only shared on a need-to-know basis, but I'll venture a guess you've already surpassed that status." He chuckled at that, and I joined in. Maybe we could be friends after all.

My thoughts returned to the combat training and Krav Maga.

"Wait, I'm curious about something. Krav Maga is a modern Israeli martial art form. How is it that the Aztec's are training in this method?"

Vital looked at me with a puzzled expression.

"The warriors don't train in this form, we do. I suppose we could teach them, but I'm not sure the gods would be thrilled with us changing the course of Aztec history."

"What do you mean?"

"We trained Krav Maga before we were sent here. I guess they haven't shared many details about our training with you, or the others yet. I'm sure they'd rather not remember... our failure." He said looking down at the ground as I sensed his grief.

Sent here? Their training? Failure?

"The Calpulli haven't shared the details of our mission. They're keeping me... us, in the dark," I said, realizing I couldn't continue being cautious in my questioning. I simply didn't have time.

"Okay, I'll tell you, if you must know. Everyone was sure we were the much anticipated Linx. The four of us met on a Saturday afternoon, in a street market here in this city, in our world known as Mexico City. We were accompanied by our handlers and instructed not to say a word until we were in a safe place. We simply sized each other up." He smiled before continuing. "Isaiah and I seemed to have an immediate bond. He was the one trained in Krav Maga, a master black belt. His father was an elite special operative in the Israeli military who taught his son everything he knew." His expression grew somber. Questions welled up in me, but I had a suspicion he would tell me more without being pressured.

"We lived in a historic district of the city, known as San Angel. Not sure if it's still the same in your time, but in our time, the 1950's, it was as if every tree and stone spoke to us." He gazed off into the distance, as he remembered that time. "It was a disaster. My stubbornness is what got Isaiah killed. We never had a chance. He was the most well-versed in combat, and the enemy knew it. They went for the weakest, which was me. I walked right into their trap," His words choked off as he swallowed hard.

"I've had plenty of time to reflect since then. I became obsessed with hand to hand combat training. I've learned many secrets of the art of combat. The gods seem pleased, but I sense they still hold a grudge."

Vitale looked at me, "Now it's up to you and your Linx. You must lead them to victory. Failure is not an option."

At that moment Tadeo approached. Vitale snapped to attention, and I attempted to follow his lead.

Tadeo did not look pleased as he carefully stepped around us. I tried to guess what he was thinking. I dared not look in Vitale's direction as my insides churned. My heart was thumping so hard I was sure it would be visible through my top. Even as I felt Tadeo's menacing presence, I noticed Elisha standing off to one side. He only winked at me with a sympathetic smile.

I had been holding my breath, but finally remembered to gulp in some air which almost caused me to pass out. *Ah well what does it matter*, I thought, *it's only a dream anyway. Any minute now I'll wake up in my bedroom on Capitol Hill, under leaden gray skies, dreading going to school.*

At that moment, a vision of my mother flashed through my mind. I recognized my need to capture life's moments as they happen. That's what Mom would want. I was ready to move on, but still hoping this was all just a dream. At the same time, I recognized the need to live my life as it happens.

Just then Tadeo came to stand directly in front of me, purposely invading my space. Little did he know the only place I wanted to be at that moment was far away from him, in a time where none of this existed. I took momentary pleasure in the thought that all of this might be just a bad dream. The knowledge that he could not control my mind made me even happier, as I let my thoughts wander back to many evenings filled with juvenile antics. Not this solitude or silent monotony...nothing about saving the world or prophecies that led to special powers.

His mood shifted slightly as he dared a smile, a hint that he actually cared. My heart skipped a beat and my instincts kicked in as I challenged him with a look of defiance. I refused to allow myself to be carried away by my feelings for him. To be honest, though, something about him made me yearn for his touch, his warmth, and I just wanted to close my eyes and feel his lips on mine.

Those thoughts awakened a flame that had lain dormant, within me. He was simply beautiful, much more beautiful than I felt was fair.

Struggling against my secret urges, I tried to look away but only succeeded in becoming more exhilarated by his presence. Common sense deserted me, as the flames rose from within, accompanied by a certain cynicism as I toyed with the element that now engulfed my entire body.

It was time to show him I wasn't weak as I circled

him like prey. He simply stood there unwavering.

Elisha and Vitale took a few cautious steps back, and the other warriors followed suit. I snickered at their retreat.

From now on my training would be on my terms. There would be no holding back, of information, nor techniques. No more secrets. After all, they needed me more than I needed them. If they couldn't appreciate me, I'd simply refuse to engage. Childish? Perhaps. But it seemed that down every path lay more secrets, and I would no longer remain in the shadows.

CHAPTER SIXTEEN

"Is this some kind of a game to you? The world needs the protection of a warrior, not a foolish girl," Tadeo challenged me with a fierce glare as I continued to circle him, allowing my flames to grow. "Need I remind you, you've only just discovered your element, and still have no control over it?"

I felt like laughing out loud, but I thought it might come across as a bit too psychotic and a desperate cry for attention. Instead, I surrounded him in a controlled circle of flames, just so he'd know I was serious. He was right, this was no longer a game.

"Since the moment I met you, you've done nothing but feed me half-truths.' I cried, "It stops right now! I'm tired of all these messed up mind games everyone keeps playing with me. Why don't you start telling me the truth, at least your version of the truth and how I fit into all of this?" I allowed the flames to subside slightly, giving him a chance to realize this was not a game, at least not for me.

He stood there staring at me, unwilling to compromise his position. Tlacateccatl...The General...The Shorn One... The Warrior.

I stared back at him equally defiant. I could be as unbending as he could, maybe even more.

The sun crept slowly above the horizon, its golden rays caressing my skin, sending pulses of energy through my veins. My heart was nearly bursting out of my chest, and for the first time in a long time, I felt alive...truly alive. Gulping in deep breaths of the fragrant morning air, I faced the rising sun and began to truly understand my connection to this magnificent fireball. Perhaps the reason my element hadn't felt so alive before now, was because in Seattle, the sky is often overcast, and whenever I'd been in this place and time, it had been mostly at night. At this moment, and this place, I was no longer going to hold back. It felt good.

My whole being radiated the sun's warmth. I was on fire. I felt like singing one of my mom's favorite jams 'This Girl Is On Fire!' However, I was sure no one here would find it amusing, or even know what it was. So, I merely allowed myself a small chuckle as I soaked up the heat, my arms open wide, in complete and utter bliss!

I'd almost forgotten about Tadeo when I noticed a

crowd of onlookers had gathered. Several of Tadeo's warriors formed a circle around us in a stance I wasn't familiar with. Vitale and Elisha were in the lead, seeming more at ease than the rest. Tadeo continued staring at me, more annoyed than I could remember.

It seemed I'd played the foolish girl part too well.

As I let my flames die down, Tadeo motioned for me to follow him. We didn't speak, and I noticed Vitale and Elisha following behind us, with two or three other warriors. I was paying little attention to the direction we were headed, but followed obediently, somewhat mortified.

Had I only imagined everything that had happened back there? Had no one noticed me standing there in flames? Good grief, how embarrassing…they all must've thought I was absolutely crazy? How was I supposed to come here to train and be taken seriously if I was going to be having outbursts like that? I just wanted to go home.

Unfortunately, going home was totally beyond my control.

When we came to a halt, and I glanced around, I had no idea where we were. I did know it was a place I'd never seen before. We were now on a high, wide open plateau. Full daybreak was upon us, and there was almost no ground cover. Many guards and warriors were gathered for training, and most seemed to be enjoying themselves immensely. Vitale broke away as we moved on a little further to gain distance from the others, then when he rejoined us, he was carrying weapons. I recognized all of them immediately.

Tadeo had reached his breaking point with me. He'd given me the courtesy of training in privacy with the more elite warriors, but now he was no longer concerned with this. He had chosen to subject me to the openness of training with any Tom, Dick, or Harry. I suppose I deserved it.

If that's what I need to do to regain the warrior's respect, I will do it without complaint. In the end, what really matters is the training. That was our mission. I resolved not to lose focus again. *Vitale is right, no more distractions.*

As we reached a level area, Tadeo snapped some instructions to his warriors, and they broke off into small training groups. Everyone had their orders, and Vitale's were to take me off to a far corner and restart my training. No audience, thank goodness, but no leniency either. He was to train me as one would train any new warrior, he informed me.

I understood then why it was Vitale who was chosen to train me. Unlike Elisha, Vitale had a vendetta. He saw me as the only person who could avenge his friend. Vitale would ensure my skills were lethal in counterattacking.

He started by warming me up, going over the basics again. He wasn't afraid to engage me with force and offered no apologies. He reminded me that the enemy wouldn't be apologetic or forgiving.

I grunted and yelped as I was thrown to the ground more times than I cared to count. "Protect your head.

You're letting your guard down," he repeated for the umpteenth time. We sparred nonstop with no breaks for water even though my throat was parched from all the heavy breathing. My legs were reasonably strong, but my upper body was weak, and he took full advantage of the fact.

Tears mingled with sweat and ran down my face, but I didn't stop. Ollin and Zoe's faces flashed before me. If I couldn't get through this for myself, I would do it for them.

As I searched my mind looking for all the reasons I needed to find strength to continue, I suddenly stopped and stepped back. *Krav Maga*. When Vitale had related his story, those words had sounded familiar. But I hadn't remembered why, until now.

Vitale commanded me to step back up. I refused.

"I just remembered something. My mother studied Krav Maga. I had forgotten that until now. I think she was a black belt." I tried to jog my memory some more, wishing I had paid more attention. But it was something she had done when I was away at school.

"Isn't she dead? How's she supposed to train you if she's dead?"

I wasn't sure how he knew this information, nor why he was so insensitive in his mention of it. I decided not to dwell on it, though, especially considering what had led me to be training in this particular place.

"Yes, it's true she's dead. I've never mentioned it to anyone here. How did you know?" I fixed my eyes on him as I waited for a reply.

I could tell He was trying to maintain his composure, but I caught him glancing towards Tadeo, who was busy training with Elisha. "I'm not sure. You must have mentioned it to someone, most likely Tadeo. Anyway, I learned that your mother had passed away. My apologies if you were trying to keep it a secret. Perhaps we should take a water break."

He walked away toward a group of warriors. I took my time heading for the water bucket and thinking to myself. *I could train in Krav Maga in my own time with both Zoe and Ollin. Also, I need to figure out how on earth Vitale knew about my mother, and who else knows, and what else do they know that they're keeping from me? More importantly, will I be sore and bruised when I wake up?*

When I reached the others, Vitale made a point of ignoring me. Elisha and Tadeo and a few others had followed us toward the water bucket. It seemed we'd started a trend.

Elisha seemed to be the only one of the two interested in talking to me. After some brief small talk, I asked him if he also knew about my mother's death. He looked surprised, "No I didn't know. I'm sorry to hear that." He made a point of not prying further and didn't inquire how she'd died.

I watched Tadeo's jaw clench when the topic came up and noticed him glancing directly at Vitale, who in turn avoided eye contact with him. I found this encounter very interesting. *That's how he knows.* I didn't even notice I was giving automatic answers to Elisha's questions because I was so focused on the interaction between Tadeo and Vitale. Something about my mother's death was causing tension between the two of them. I needed to find out why.

I was jolted back to my conversation with Elisha when I realized he was pressing me for further information about Sporadic Fatal Insomnia.

I gave him a deer in the headlights look which caused him to hesitate for a moment, "So are you going to explain it to me? What exactly is Sporadic Fatal Insomnia?"

I gasped, in surprise. How could I have gone this far without even noticing what I was saying? I opened my mouth and closed it again. The words simply wouldn't come, but I felt the tears on the verge of breaking out. I wouldn't allow it, not again. I took a deep trembling breath, and then another.

Tadeo was suddenly at my side, his hand on my arm as he gently pulled me away. As soon as we'd gained a little distance, he released my arm.

"I'm sorry you were forced to discuss a topic so personal and so obviously painful. I'm not sure how Vitale found out, but I can assure you it was not from me. I did know about it, however. I've known since before you first arrived here." He stopped in his tracks and looked down at me. "Both Nahui Atl and I were made aware of the situation at the same time. My only guess is that Vitale somehow found out while we were in the temple. Please allow me to investigate further. I will get to the bottom of it. In the meantime, I need you to remain focused. Every moment lost here is a moment those demons gain." He looked back, towards the others. It no longer mattered to me. My mission was very clear. Training was the prime objective.

Tears rolled down my cheeks, and I did nothing to stop them. They spoke the truth that had been plaguing me for so long. Pain that I had been trying to hide, and fear I'd been avoiding. Allowing myself to cry out every single emotion I'd held in for so long, my body shook with my sobs, and I felt Tadeo take me into his arms. His gesture only served to open the floodgates, and I cried harder.

What new trials lie ahead for me? As the tears flowed, that question echoed deep down inside.

CHAPTER SEVENTEEN

I gradually wiped the tears from my face, as my sobbing subsided. The saltiness already burned as I attempted to leave no trace of wetness behind.

I jumped with a start when a hand began gently stroking my hair.

Looking up, I encountered a pair of obsidian eyes, which held me and pulled me in.

Together, Zoe and I were immediately transported to an ocean, cool and teeming with life. Our bodies became synchronized as we swam in the depths. A huge array of sea life gave way to us as if welcoming us. Deeper and deeper we went.

Suddenly the water around us was brightly illuminated, and I looked over at my companion, startled by what was happening. There was no doubt where the bright, captivating light was coming from as my companion's body was now engulfed in it. We continued to descend, deeper and deeper still.

I couldn't help smiling and thinking, what strange world are we a part of now?

I ventured to take a deep breath, and at that very moment, I awoke, only to find Zoe sitting in the same place in the closet I'd seen her last.

I attempted to stand too quickly and grimaced in pain at the head rush. I thought back to my rough training with Vitale. Zoe was studying me carefully, probably wondering what was going on. And then it occurred to me, *I need to figure out how to explain Krav Maga to her and Ollin.*

First, though, I needed to discover if Zoe knew I had just connected with her, in my dream state.

"What happened to me...did I pass out?" I asked innocently at first. It was probably just a matter of time before someone would come looking for us. I wasn't even sure how long we'd been away from the others.

"You did. I think it's normal if you can call it that, when we start using our powers. Our bodies become drained easily. As we grow more used to it, it should happen less and less."

"Before you say anything, that was me with you. I pulled you into my place of escape, the ocean." She stroked her long hair as she rose and moved to leave the closet. "I have no way of explaining it, so I had to show you. No one else knows about it, and I'd like to keep it that way, for now. At least until I fully understand the meaning of this dream travel, or dream-scaping as I've come to call it."

"Zoe, wait!" She stopped at the urgency in my voice. "Have you ever heard of Krav Maga?"

"It's a self-defence technique, right? Some form of martial art?"

"I think it could be key to success in our impending battles. The idea came to me when I was training in the dream state."

Zoe moved to open the door. "Let me approach the group about it, maybe I'll start with Ollin." I nodded in agreement.

When we rejoined the others downstairs, there was an ominous tension in the air. Zoe sensed it as well, as we both quickly scanned the room. Ollin and Mr. Anderson were missing, and Alasdair wore a very unpleasant scowl on his face. It didn't take a rocket scientist to figure the source of the tension.

A familiar voice echoed from out in the hall. I turned to look at Zoe, who rolled her eyes. She didn't seem surprised as Mr. Caberletti entered the room.

"There the two of you are!" He exclaimed, rather cheerfully. Cheerfulness was decidedly something we weren't accustomed to, coming from him.

"No need to be alarmed Viviana, I too am part of the Capulli." He winked as he said it.

Good grief, things were becoming even more complicated. Flustered, I made my way out to the back patio, paying no attention to anyone else.

Outdoors once again, the evening was settling in. Neighing and canting of horses could be heard in the distance. The trees provided a sanctuary of sorts, a comforting feeling. As I wandered through the garden, my thoughts were focused on the fourth Linx. *Who could it possibly be? Where will we find the fourth elemental? Do the others have any clues they've been keeping from us?*

Turning to face the back of the house, I observed Alasdair's silhouette staring out into the garden. I first thought he was looking at me, except he was obviously lost in thought. Recognizing this, I allowed him his space, as I moved toward the side gardens.

Earth Linx. Who are you and where were we going to find you?

As I re-entered the house, it became clear that some sort of disagreement had been going on. Humberto was attempting to reason with Alasdair, who was visibly upset. Ollin was only a few steps away, looking very aggressive. Mr. Anderson seemed to be holding him back. *What in the world has happened?*

As I approached Zoe, I could tell she was rather enjoying whatever squabble had or was about to take place. I also noticed my father and Citlali observing from a corner of the room. The expression on my father's face was of utmost concern, while Citlali seemed just as amused as Zoe.

Humberto was insisting on allowing someone to test Alasdair, but I wasn't sure what sort of testing he was referring to. Ollin let out a rather obnoxious laugh.

Alasdair seemed to be fighting the urge to punch his brother.

There was a strange energy in the room. Sort of like my fire element, only this wasn't coming from me. Without thinking about it, I moved towards Alasdair. Something was drawing me to him. In what seemed to be a rather bold move, I reached out a hand to touch his. Once again, a huge spark ignited between the two of us. I was overcome with awe, as I stood motionless, feeling the surge transcend me.

The entire room fell silent.

Alasdair locked eyes with mine. Those ice blue eyes looked lethal, but I didn't flinch. I gazed back at him with equal intensity.

"Satisfied?" His words cut like a knife. "I'm only human, sorry. Oh, and yes, my element is stronger than it should be. They call them powers?" He took in a deep breath. "I call it a curse."

Pulling away from Humberto, Alasdair bolted for the front door. Moments later the engine of his McLaren roared to life. We all remained quiet, listening to the sound of his engine fading into the distance.

A sudden sadness overcame me. He'd said his powers were a curse. And what had he meant by stronger than it should be? Finally, Ollin broke the silence.

"He's stronger than he led us to believe." His voice seemed cautious as he walked away from Mr. Anderson. No one else spoke for several minutes. I'd totally forgotten Mr. Caberletti was among us until he broke the silence.

"In all my years as a Capulli I've never heard of this, but we're still not clear how strong his powers are. We must test him as soon as possible." He seemed to be talking more to himself than anyone else.

Zoe spoke up then, "Considering he just stormed off, I'd say that testing will have to wait until he returns. If he returns?" It was then I realized this must've been the source of the tension. Ollin must've outed him. His own brother. But why? More questions, and still no answers. Looking over at my father and Citlali, I discovered the two of them observing me closely. I was suddenly uncomfortable and smiled nervously at them. My father's face warmed up enough to return the gesture. For a moment, I allowed myself to study his features carefully. I had done this often since Mamá had passed away. Life seemed too fragile, to take things or people for granted. I didn't want to forget his features, ever.

Whenever I tried to remember her, and I was nowhere near a photo, I found myself yearning for the tiny details of her face that I'd never really taken the time to appreciate, to love. I was scared I'd wake up one day unable to remember her face at all, I'd once panicked during a car ride. Jim had pulled over on the shoulder of the freeway, immediately joining me in the back seat, to offer whatever comfort he could.

Later that week, when I climbed into the back seat of the car, I found a small ornate box. I'd looked up at him in the rear-view mirror, and he'd simply smiled. Opening the box, I found a gold locket and chain, but the most precious memento was in the locket, a carefully cut out photo of my mother. He'd made sure I'd never be fearful of forgetting what she looked like again.

I made my way towards my dad. It seemed like the right time for a hug, not that I ever needed a right moment. It felt like he needed it as well, as he took in a rather deep breath, releasing it slowly. I knew this to be a habit of his, either when he was stressed or holding back tears.

I caught sight of Zoe out of the corner of my eye, watching us, and then her gaze shifted to her father, who didn't seem phased in the slightest. Once again, I was overcome by an overwhelming sadness that made me want to embrace her. Zoe might come across as strong and resilient, but having never known her mother, and her father being absent most of the time, it was no wonder she was a bit callous.

"Sorry to be the one to interrupt the moment, but we really need to discuss a few things," Citlali – Nahui – Lady of the Jade Skirts said. Once again, there was that fragrance that drew me in. And her voice. Something about her voice was so soothing to me.

Zoe turned her full attention to Citlali, as did Ollin. I knew no one else understood what was happening, but I had a very strong inclination. Nahui had the power to control the emotions of mere mortals and command our attention.

"We have much to discuss, and I need all of you to focus on this mission from here on. The three of you have a lot to learn, and very little time in which to do it. Not only that, we still must locate the fourth Linx."

I was so glad the topic of the fourth Linx had finally come up.

"Before we get into the logistics of how all this is going to work around your school schedules, we need to discuss the past." She glanced furtively in Humberto's direction. *I wonder what that's about?*

"Wait! What? School? How on earth do you expect us to go to school in the midst of all this?" Zoe was beyond peeved, and I didn't blame her. Apparently, that part had gone right over my head.

Ollin let out a grunt, as he pushed his fingers through his hair. "Seriously, school? I'm with Zoe on this one. No way, no how."

Closely monitoring my counterparts, and the expressions of the others, I decided to wait to say my piece. I was interested in learning how this was going to be instrumental to the mission.

"Yes, school. Not just for appearances, but also because at the end of the day you're still teenagers and even Linx have to go to school," said Mr. Anderson. His stance and expression left no doubt that he was indeed Zoe's father. *How much alike these two actually are*, I thought to myself as I held back a smile.

Zoe challenged her father, accusing him of possibly being at the center of this ill-conceived idea, simply to torment her. They exchanged a few miserable glares, but in the end, it was Zoe who conceded. Ollin went to her side, in an attempt to comfort her, but Zoe tensed at his presence, a clear signal for him to back off.

I turned my focus back to Citlali, reassuring her I was still listening, and interested in hearing more.

"School, yes. For several reasons, including those Mr. Anderson just cited, which are important. However, there is a school not far from here with a well-kept secret. When the school was built, a member of the Calpulli was the head of the oversight committee. With the Tetrad Prophecy in mind, the Calpulli sent in a special team to build the gym." Citlali seemed quite proud to be sharing this news with us as she continued. "This property has direct underground access to that gym, and therefore, into the school."

"Wait, are we talking about Kentwood High School? You're not suggesting we transfer to a public school?" I shocked even myself with my hostile reaction. As if this entire prophecy and its mission weren't enough, they expected us to transfer to a new high school, in the middle of the school year. The thought terrified me. Literally shaken, I turned to my father who offered his best fatherly look of reassurance. But he wasn't fooling me. He had to think the idea was ludicrous. You don't pluck a teenager out of one school and drop them into a new one, especially not in their junior year of high school. That was like feeding us to the barracudas.

"Do you all understand how insane this is?" Pausing, I made eye contact with each adult in that room. "You expect us to agree to this with no resistance? If that's the case, you are all wildly out of your minds. I'm not doing it." My eyes watered beyond my control. Attempting to hold back as best as I could, I continued. "The moment they find out Zoe and I come from JPA, they'll eat us alive and spit us out. You can't do this to us. You're asking too much. I will not agree to it." And just like that, I broke down.

In all honesty, school was the last thing on my mind, and a new school was not an option.

My father offered me comfort, as Humberto moved in closer. I stared him square in the face. "You come back now, and bring all this chaos with you?" My words were sharp. They were intended to hurt.

"Viviana Magnus. That's enough!" My father sternly reprimanded me. Perhaps I deserved it. But was I lying? Had he not turned my world upside down with his arrival?

Pinching off my tears, yet angry and hurt, I sulked in my defeat.

"I'm sorry to cause you pain, Vivi, I truly am. I wish this all could be different, that you wouldn't have to be involved. But you are. You're at the very center of it. If I could change places with you, I would gladly." I knew my uncle spoke the truth. He looked upset with himself, even ill. I felt a tad awful, but just a tad. I was still angry at him for everything, but mostly for not being there when I needed him.

Citlali must have been working her tricks again, as a sudden familiar calmness crept over me. I glanced at her, and she offered a friendly smile.

"OK, let's say we go to this school. What's the main purpose, aside from the gym? I mean we can access the gym without needing to even step foot in the actual school." Zoe didn't seem concerned for the same reasons I did. Or maybe she just hid it much better. I mean, how could she even consider the possibility, so quickly?

It was Mr. Caberletti who offered a response. "Allow me to answer that question." He cleared his throat as he proceeded. "We have no way of detecting the goddesses, but if history tells us anything, they will come in a form similar to the Linx. Meaning, they will come in teenage form, and will do their best to get as close to all of you as possible."

"You are offering us up as bait? Is that what you're saying?" Ollin, like myself, suddenly looked and sounded horrified.

"We need you all to calm down and listen. Just hear us out, would you please?" That was Mr. Caberletti's assertive voice. I'd heard it many times in class. He proceeded, "This is why we are here. We don't have much time, and as Citlali has already mentioned, we still need to locate the fourth Linx. So work with us here. Please."

"Do we have any other options?" Zoe rudely demanded.

"As a matter of fact, you do. You each have the option to say no. It will not stop us from trying, but the likelihood of anyone but the Elemental Linx succeeding is not good." Taking a deep controlled breath, he continued. "I don't like that we have put so much of a burden on four teenagers, who are just beginning to live and enjoy life. But I didn't have a say in the prophecy. My job, the Calpulli's job is to protect the prophecy, to protect you." He made a fist and sighed. "We need them to come to you. So yes, as frightening as it may sound, you need to lure them in, on your own territory and your own terms. Which is why training is of the utmost importance, as is locating the Earth Linx."

His words resonated with me. Back in Tenochtitlan, the stress had been on my training. And once again, Krav Maga was at the center of my thoughts, as was Tadeo.

"Krav Maga. We need to learn Krav Maga." I blurted out. Zoe gave me an angry glare, but I didn't care. My focus once again was clear. We needed to train.

CHAPTER EIGHTEEN

Everyone had been settled into comfortable sleeping arrangements. The men, with the exception of Ollin, had been installed in the guest house. The master bedroom, which had been my parent's room, remained empty. I suspected my father couldn't bring himself to stay there. He'd offered the room to Citlali, but she opted for the guest room which connected her to Zoe's room via a Jack & Jill bathroom. Zoe didn't seem thrilled about it, but she couldn't very well admit to it.

The night's silence was welcoming, at least until I heard a car pulling into the driveway. Jumping out of bed, I ran to the window. A white car was creeping slowly toward the house with its light off, like a pale ghost in the darkness.

Alasdair.

Unsure why his arrival was causing knots in my stomach, I quickly retreated into the darkest part of the room, afraid he might've spotted me. Then it dawned on me, he would need access to the house, so I rushed down to let him in through the garage.

As Alasdair exited the vehicle gracefully and walked in my direction, I fought to keep my knees from caving in on me.

"Thank you, Viviana. Did I wake you?" His voice was more relaxed than I'd remembered.

Fidgeting with the hem of my top I said, "No, I was still awake." As I moved back through the house, he followed me.

I explained the sleeping arrangements to him and asked if he wanted anything from the kitchen, but he politely declined.

I was about to excuse myself when he surprised me by asking if we could talk. Hesitantly, I nodded agreement and moved toward the dining room. It seemed like the most appropriate place to have a conversation. It would allow me to keep a little distance between us by sitting across the table from him. It seemed necessary at that moment in time.

I honestly had no idea why, but Alasdair made me uneasy. I felt like I needed to hold myself back in his presence.

The new moon illuminated the room, making it unnecessary to turn on the light.

"Sorry for bolting out of here the way I did. It was rude and childish." He said, as I carefully studied his features. Alasdair was a very handsome man. His eyes shone like pale topaz even in the dimly lit room. Absolutely beautiful.

I replied coyly. "I wouldn't say childish. It seems you too are dealing with some issues." He simply sat there with a blank look, so I continued. "I'm not going to ask you any questions. You either want to share, or you don't, it's up to you. Let's just agree not to touch, because whatever it is that you've got going on doesn't seem to mesh well with me." I chuckled, and he smiled sheepishly.

"I'm sorry about that. I'm not exactly sure what the connection or disconnect with our elements is, but rest assured, the Calpulli will do whatever is necessary to figure it out." He winked at me, and I had no reason not to believe him.

"I went up to the pass to cool down," he laughed, "the average person would be afraid of bears, or mountain lions up there, things like that. But I was afraid of something far worse, Aztec deities."

I let out a nervous laugh. I knew I was the one the deities were looking for.

I filled him in on the evening's events as he sat quietly, taking it all in. Well at least until I pressed him for his thoughts on the subject.

"That would mean I'll have to attend school as well." He looked right past me, staring out of the window.

"Why? How old are you Alasdair?"

"I'm 17, almost 18." *That would make him a senior. Why wouldn't he be going to school with us?* I asked myself.

"Ollin and I were educated in Europe, and I've already graduated," he explained. "But I imagine the Calpulli will send me to the school anyway, mostly as additional protection for the rest of you.

I allowed that to sink in. He and Ollin were only months apart. Not even a full year. He seemed to have read my mind.

"Yes, Ollin and I are nine months apart." He smiled as if remembering something. "My parents were apparently deeply in love, and I don't mean that as a joke." He fell silent.

We maintained the silence for a few minutes until I blurted out, "So what happened? To your parents, I mean?"

A wave of painful sorrow overcame me at that moment. Unsure of the source, I stood to my feet. "Would you care to accompany me out to the back deck for a bit of fresh air?" Alasdair nodded in agreement and followed me out.

As we stepped out of the heat of the house, I took a few deep breaths and almost immediately felt the heaviness leave my body. Along with that came a huge sense of relief.

"Are you OK?" He inquired.

"Yes. I apologize. I'm not sure what came over me. But whatever it was is gone now." I assured him.

He smiled warmly, which sent a different feeling through me, but I immediately suppressed it.

"My parents. You want to know what happened." He shoved his hands deep into his pockets, "Our mom passed away during childbirth, Ollin's obviously." He looked away for a moment, which caused me to regret my prying. "Our father was killed in an automobile accident. But the Calpulli believe it was no accident. The deities were after him, tracking us down. He'd gone to great lengths to erase any connections with us. We would only meet up with him under the protection of the Calpulli. It wasn't the best of circumstances, but it worked for a while."

"He was a great father, who did everything he could to ensure our happiness and safety." The sincerity in his voice overwhelmed me. It had never occurred to me what dangers our parents could be in.

As I moved to sit down, something occurred to me. *Their mother died during childbirth just as Zoe's had. Was that just a coincidence?* The thought bothered me. But I wouldn't say anything just now. I would look further into it later and tucked it away in the back of my mind.

A sudden breeze passed over us sending chills up and down my spine. I looked up towards the window of Ollin's room to try and determine if he was the cause, but his room was in darkness.

Alasdair glanced in the same direction and immediately stepped to my side. "That's not a friendly." His voice remained calm, yet with a hard edge, as his eyes surveyed the surrounding property. "Quickly, go inside." He commanded in a low voice.

At that, my element came alive. Taking a deep breath, I followed his order, more aware of my internal flame than ever.

He followed me inside, closed the door, and moved away from it, all in one motion. Then he reached for the cell phone in his back pocket.

"We've got an unfriendly here. I'm not sure if it's on the property or not, but it's in the area at least." He listened to the response and disconnected.

"Who'd you call?" I assumed it was one of the adults. But I still wanted to know.

"Your Uncle Humberto."

There was a sudden rattling noise against one of the windows. It was just like during a windstorm, except there wasn't any wind at the moment.

Terror overcame me, as a screeching sound like fingernails on a blackboard pierced the air. Something cast a shadow over the windows, blocking out the moonlight and Alasdair pulled me with him into the hallway, placing a finger to his lips, indicating the need for silence.

My element was fighting its way up from deep within me, but I knew giving it free rein would be dangerous, so I did my best to suppress it.

More windows rattled, and the screeching sound came again. Nearly petrified, I listened intently, noting the precise locations in the house the noises were coming from. That way I would know where not to run if the need arose.

Down the hall, the light of the moon appeared and disappeared from view. Something was lurking out there. Whatever it was – was large enough to block a considerable amount of the moonlight.

My heart was beating wildly. I knew I wasn't ready to face an enemy, not yet, not without training. If I did, I was pretty sure I would die. Closing my eyes, all I could see with my inner vision was Micteca and Coyolxa. I'd gotten a good look at them before, so I knew exactly who I was facing. Still, knowing didn't make it any better or make me any braver.

As visions of possible outcomes raced through my head, I felt a hand squeeze mine. That's when I realized I was holding Alasdair's hand and had been digging my nails into his palm.

His thumb was stroking the top of my hand, providing reassurance, or maybe trying to remind me that he too felt pain.

Immediately, I pulled my hand away, too embarrassed to read his reaction. I turned to focus my attention back towards the only windows from which we could still see moonlight.

Ominous shadows still shifted out there as the fire inside me readied itself for combustion. I could feel the energy reaching all the way out to my fingertips, but I continued to hold it at bay.

Suddenly, I was overcome by a terrible headache. An enormous pressure built inside my head, as I fought back nausea that brought me to my knees. Pressing my palms over my ears, I rested my forehead on the floor and fought the urge to vomit.

Alasdair was at my side, saying something, but I couldn't make out the words. A taunting laugh that I know I'd heard before, overwhelmed me, causing even more pain, if that were possible.

"You are not beyond my reach. We'll find you *Tletl*. Your fire will soon burn out." It was Coyolxa as I'd suspected all along.

Continuing to strain against my element, I pressed my hands over my ears even tighter.

I felt Alasdair's hand on my back, and at that moment it occurred to me I'd held his hand earlier, and nothing unusual had happened, no sparks, nothing. Latching onto that thought seemed to help ease my nausea, so I focused on his hand resting there along my spine. Again, the mocking laughter spread through my head, and my chest began to ache with loathing.

Exhausted from holding back, I hit the floor with my fists as sparks ignited all around me. My element was smoldering, as I cast flames from my fingertips. The pressure in my head quickly subsided.

Alasdair stood directly in front of me, his blue eyes electrifying as I took advantage of the moment to look deeper into them. There was something very peculiar about his eyes. They seemed to be giving off some sort of energy. As I reached out to touch his face, a spark exploded in the air. His element, unlike mine, looked like tiny thunderbolts. A loud crackling echoed throughout the house as our elements collided.

I'd never felt so alive, as I reined my element in.

The moon once more illuminated the entire hall, without interference. The house was quiet again, but yet, Alasdair and I remained exactly where we were.

Both of us jumped at the sound of a door opening. Well, I jumped behind Alasdair, and he simply accommodated me. Then the hushed voice of my father, and the footsteps of the others entering the room caused us both to relax.

My eyes were well adjusted to the dark, and as soon as I made out Dad's silhouette, I rushed to him, and he welcomed me into his arms.

"Oh sweetie, I'm so sorry I wasn't here for you. Are you two okay?" He asked.

"No, I'm not okay. I was terrified. Those two lunatics found me, and in my own home of all places." I complained.

How was I supposed to feel? But I was also excited by the encounter I'd just had with Alasdair's element.

As my father held me, my body stiffened, and my breathing became shallow, though I was trying desperately to fill my lungs. The hallway light went on, which caused my vision to be clouded with dark spots. I was losing control, and I was hyperventilating.

I could hear Dad calling my name, but it sounded distant, and I was too weak to respond. Slowly, I drifted into a deep slumber, only this time I knew it would lead me straight to Tadeo.

* * *

When I awoke, I knew instantly where I was. Out

of instinct, I sat up knowing I was not alone. Sure enough, there were guards in the distance, and Elisha sat there observing me with a huge smile on his face.

My thoughts wandered back home, and what had happened there mere minutes before.

"The goddesses found me," I whispered to Tadeo as I stood up.

He didn't flinch, as a matter of fact, he made no indication he'd even heard.

I brushed earth from my clothes, as I was about to repeat myself, but he stopped me with a nod indicating he had heard and started to walk away. Just like that, we'd resumed our routine of me following where he chose to lead. Taking in my surroundings, I looked for recognizable landmarks but gave up quickly. Nothing was familiar, with the exception of the rhythm we always seemed to fall into during my visits.

This time the walk seemed to take us much farther. The pace didn't bother me, as a matter of fact, it felt good, as head gradually cleared.

A wide variety of vegetation surrounded us, and out of it all, I recognized a beautiful scent, the same scent Citlalli wore. It had to be coming from the flowers beside the path, the same flowers she'd worn in her hair when I'd first met her in the underground temple.

I was so busy looking around I was startled back to the present when I bumped into Tadeo's back because he'd stopped suddenly. His body was very solid, and his bare back damp with a sheen of sweat. I was too embarrassed to wipe his sweat from my face for fear he'd see me as too girly, so I simply stepped to the side, trying to ignore my stumble. Tadeo certainly didn't seem phased.

Once again, we'd arrived at what appeared to be yet another training ground. This one was tucked neatly away, surrounded by overgrown forest. There were fewer warriors here, and the ones who were seemed to be more of the elite type. These were the ones that had been with Tadeo when we'd confronted the lunatic goddesses.

I glance around curiously then spotted Vitale. He was engaged in serious combat with three other men. They all seemed extremely skilled, but Vitale held his own quite well. I was impressed and felt honored to be his pupil.

Tadeo brought me back to reality, "You may join Vitale and his group for today's instruction."

* * *

As I went down yet again, I grunted angrily and pulled myself up for the umpteenth time. Vitale scornfully reminded me that the deities would have no mercy, nor would they wait for me to get back on my feet. I despised him with every ounce of my being at that moment, as I tried to push on. However, I soon found out I was beyond physical exhaustion. *Must fight harder*, I told myself. But my body quickly reminded me that I was still only a seventeen-year-old girl.

With one grand sweep Vitale had me on the ground again. A wail of pain and frustration escaped me, as tears flooded my eyes.

I kept reminding myself I needed to be strong and find his weak spot. Warding him off as best I could, I studied his movements. He appeared to be favoring his left side, which made sense since he was a leftie, but then I realized he seemed to be protecting his lower rib area on that side. *Very interesting.*

The very next time Vitale attempted to pull me down, I raised my leg and delivered a mighty roundhouse kick, right in that lower rib area. For once I had caught him by surprise. He grunted in pain, his left hand going immediately to the area of impact. He hunched over, one knee on the ground with a grimace of pain on his face. All he said to me was, "It's about time."

I stood a bit taller then, as I indulged myself in my small sense of accomplishment.

"I think we've earned a rest," he said, and we slowly made our way towards the water bucket at the edge of the clearing.

Indeed, I truly needed the break. Water had never tasted or felt so good in my life.

"So, are you going to tell me what happened to you there?" I pointed at his left side, which he was still holding protectively.

"After our mission failed, I went on a rampage. The Calpulli moved us, till this day we still don't know where we were. I tried to escape and fell off a cliff. Broke some ribs and probably caused some internal damage, which is why it still bothers me." He smiled, as if his rebellion, despite the accident, had given him some satisfaction.

"I see. Well, I'm glad nothing more serious happened." I felt a little bad for him. It set me wondering what exactly they'd been subjected to, and how much of it any of them would share with me. At the moment, it seemed Vitale was the most willing to share, and since I'd be training with him, he seemed my only hope in learning the truth, of the other Linx mission.

We had resumed talking about the training when that familiar rumbling started again in the distance. This time it was accompanied by an awful crackling and snapping in the air around us.

The Warriors immediately took their positions, not one of them hesitated. I followed Vitale, joining up with Isaiah and Tadeo.

Tadeo was giving instructions in Nahuatl. Isaiah kindly translated for me, explaining we would be advancing toward the source. He inserted his own opinion in a low voice, validating what I'd already suspected. Coyolxa and Micteca.

We forged our way through the woods and soon arrived on the shore of a rather large lake. The Warriors took their places, as they had the last time we went into a situation such as this. Although there were fewer warriors, they were still quite intimidating to behold.

Unlike the last time, I was now much more aware of what we could be facing.

Just like the last time fog began to rise around us

blocking our vision in all directions. I stared hard into the dense fog ahead, listening intently for whatever evil lurked within. The wait made me grow impatient. I could feel my element growing stronger within me as I shifted my feet restlessly.

I sensed movement within the fog before I could actually see anything. Then gradually a silhouette materialized. It was all coming back to me now. This was how they'd appeared last time.

A chuckle escaped me. Tadeo turned to me with a questioning look, but I simply brushed him off.

Soon, my nostrils were overcome by a familiar scent. Citlalli. Without further warning, her voice was by my side.

One eyebrow raised, and a smile on her lips, "I'm glad I can join today's reunion." She was not speaking to me, or any of the warriors. As a matter of fact, she was shortening the distance between herself and the fog. That's when Micteca fully materialized, and she was exactly as I'd remembered her. There was no forgetting the platinum blonde hair and violet eyes.

"Oh, Nahui. So glad to see The Four let you off your leash, and let you come out to play."

A little confused by Micteca's words, I turned to look at Vitale, who seemed to be enjoying the exchange. Nothing, so I tried Isaiah.

"The four main gods." He whispered.

Oh yes, how could I forget them? They're the culprits responsible for all of this.

Citlalli paid no heed. If the words were meant to

hurt, they weren't doing the job. I had to admit, it was a pretty weak attempt. From what I'd witnessed thus far from Citlalli, she seemed very much in control of her emotions, considering how she seemed to be so able to control the emotions of others.

"Micteca, what brings you here today?" Straight and to the point. I liked Citlalli's style.

"You know what we seek," she turned to look at me. "That one. Give her to us, and Tecuciztecatl will not destroy the humans."

With a mere flick of a wrist, Citlalli evaporated the fog and Micteca. I was in complete awe. It was magical.

"What happened? How did you…" My thoughts simply wandered through the possibilities. This was a dream, but Citlalli existed in my real world, and I knew there, she could easily calm me. So was she also capable of this?

What world was I living in?

"Nahui, that wasn't necessary. We need to learn their intentions for the Linx, and especially for Viviana." He didn't even glance at me, his full attention was on Citlalli. I could see the tension in his jaw muscles as he spoke to her. There was a definite hierarchy, and Tadeo was obviously beneath Citlalli.

"What? Negotiate? Is that what you're suggesting Tlacateccatl? That we somehow come to a truce with them?" The irritation in her voice was apparent. He obviously noticed it as well, as he stood quietly, considering the alternatives.

CHAPTER NINETEEN

We gradually found a steady rhythm in our training, as I continued attempting to anticipate Vitale's moves. It felt hopeless, but giving up was not an option. He finally stopped to help me with my positioning. "Viviana it's important that you always anticipate your next move before you're even ready to make it."

We went over form a few times, but of course, I was a bit sloppy, so he came around behind to help align me properly, repositioning my legs and feet, tugging at my shoulders and adjusting the direction my waist needed to be in. The position felt awkward, I could feel my muscles burning, both from exhaustion and from the unfamiliar pose.

When I broke my stance, I couldn't help a low chuckle as I imagined what I'd look like just then. Vitale tried hard to hold back his own laughter but gave in finally, and we both welcomed the distraction.

I couldn't remember the last time I'd laughed so heartily. I felt a small pang, as I thought back to a day of milkshakes and hamburgers with my mom. We were trying to outdo each other with the milkshakes, and she ended up belching so loud other patrons looked at her in disgust. We laughed until we cried.

"You OK there?" Vitale inquired as he interrupted my memory.

"Yes, I'm fine. Just remembering a happy moment." I smiled.

We sat side by side, both reminiscing about private memories.

I went to wipe my face when I noticed Tadeo staring at us. It was awkward, and he quickly tried to play it off.

"So what's his deal?" I asked Vitale.

"What do you mean, his deal?" The confusion on his face reminded me how the three of them might not be familiar with current day lingo.

"Why him? Why is he the General, the Tlacateccatl, and why does he suppress his emotions so much?"

Vitale looked in Tadeo's direction as he tried to share what he knew of the General of The Shorn Ones.

They were all very young when the Calpulli brought them together. Tadeo was always the quiet one, but Isaiah seemed to get him to talk. He smiled remembering his friend. He apparently had a way about him. Tadeo's mom had just passed when they reached him. In fact, it was her passing that led them to him. Like the current Earth Linx, they had trouble locating him earlier.

"He kept pretty much to himself, but he was the absolute best during training. No one could beat him during the sparring sessions, not even Isaiah. They believed all of that raw emotion from losing his mother was released during his training, making him lethal as an opponent. However, away from the training ring, you'd never know he was the same intense opponent.

Contemplating whether I should dig any deeper, as I stared intently at Tadeo. Something about him told me there was much more beneath the surface.

Turning my attention back to Vitale, we dove right back into training. He'd also revealed that weapons training would be introduced during my next visit and that I would soon resume training with the other warriors. He didn't have to tell my how important it would be to spar with a variety of partners, to learn to read the differences in movement during combat. If I was honest with myself, I couldn't wait to get my hands on my spear.

Tadeo approached us, appearing a bit apprehensive. "It's time to get Viviana back."

How long have I been here? It seemed the longest visit so far. I was curious how we'd effect my return this time. *Will I simply lie on the ground, with everyone staring at me and go to sleep? Maybe go back to his quarters?*

"How am I going back?"

"We'll travel back to the city. Inside the temple, there's a corridor especially designed for you to travel through in situations like this."

I had to admit, the thought piqued my interest. How very adventurous and special I'd become. A snicker escaped me, which didn't seem to amuse him. I didn't I find that surprising. The ever driven and obedient Tadeo would not succumb to childish nonsense, or even indulge in any form of laughter. So I followed meekly.

The city by day was as breathtaking as it had been by night. Although the giant vases were not lit up with fire, I had a much better view of the causeways, the topography, and the people. Realizing much of the area was a grand lake, and our short canoe ride seemed to bring us to the main island.

The adults didn't seem to take any notice of us, but the children did, and they often pointed directly at me. My complexion wasn't exactly pale, but I was certainly lighter than them. Surely I wasn't that different in appearance from Tadeo, Elisha, and Vitale. They were normally lighter skinned, but they'd grown tan from training under the sun. Shaking it off, I looked around at the buildings, as we walked into a barricaded area. I hadn't remembered this from before, but then it had been dark at the time.

Finally, as we arrived at a smallish temple, the

guards disbanded, including Elisha and Vitale. I quickly reached for Vitale's hand to thank him. He gifted me with a faint smile, then cut our farewell short when he noticed Tadeo's irritation. I frankly didn't care, but then I was the one leaving, so I let it rest.

Tadeo and I proceeded through a dark passageway finally arriving in a dimly lit room. It was rather unremarkable at first sight, but there was an energy about it that beckoned me in. Tadeo stood at the doorway, reciting the method of my passage. "Walk toward the dim light at the other end of the room, call forth your element, and you'll be transported back to your time."

"Will it hurt?" I wanted to know.

"I really can't say, I've never used this mode of travel myself.

So I went toward the light, and within seconds of calling upon my inner fire, I was gone, like a puff of smoke.

* * *

When I awoke in my bed once more, only my shoes had been removed. I lay there quietly for a few moments until something stirring in the room frightened me. But then, Zoe was hushing me from close by.

"What on earth is going on with you?" A hint of worry in her voice.

"I have no idea. Wasn't it you who told me this fainting would go on until I could control my element better?" I reminded her.

"Yes, but from what I've seen you seem to be more than merely fainting," she took a seat beside me on the bed.

I sat up straightening up my hair. "How long was I out this time?" I inquired.

"Long enough. But we need to go snoop. There's something they're not telling us, and I plan on getting to the bottom of it," she hopped off the bed, impatiently waiting for me to do the same.

"What time is it?"

"The witching hour!" She said, letting out a fake evil laugh. I couldn't help it, she looked comical, so I laughed out loud in response.

We made our way down the hall. When we'd reached the top of the stairs, Ollin appeared out of nowhere, startling us both.

"What the heck Ollin! You scared me." Zoe fought to remain in control.

Ollin shushed her, ushering us both down the stairs. We complied without further comment, not wanting to wake our guests, Citlali and Alasdair.

We crossed the foyer and straight into the front study. The same one we'd ducked into upon our arrival. As I was about to turn on a lamp, Ollin stopped me.

"Why?" I asked.

"Because we don't need any unnecessary attention." He said before he quietly closed the door behind him.

Zoe took a seat behind the desk. I was surprised at

how good my night vision was, as I took one of the two seats directly across from her, and Ollin the other.

"OK. So why are the three of us down here, at 3 a.m.?" Searching their faces, I settled on Zoe's.

Ollin was the one to reply. "We believe they have an idea as to the whereabouts of the Earth Linx."

I allowed that thought to sink in for a very brief moment, as Zoe spoke.

"Ollin and I both overheard my father, Mr. Caberletti, and your uncle discussing the Earth Linx when your father and Citlali were busy tending to you. They were very careful to speak as quietly as possible, but I don't think they realized how well honed my eavesdropping skills are." She seemed rather proud of the latter.

"I think she's in Russia."

I looked to Ollin for any reaction, but when none was forthcoming, I probed. "How do you know it's a she, and that she might be in Rusia?"

She went on to explain how she heard the fourth Linx being referred to as she. However, it seemed the Russia part was a little vague. She wasn't sure if they meant she had to go through Russia, or if that was where she was located. But she was certain that the fourth Linx, the Earth Linx was a girl.

I digested the information very carefully, considering all of the potential obstacles. It seemed that regardless, this fourth Linx might not know English. That was something I hadn't considered. Communication would be key, but if one didn't understand the language, it posed the risk of setting us back.

Also, another girl. Not that I didn't believe in equal rights. But there was no denying that Ollin was certainly much stronger physically than Zoe and me. Training with Vitale had made me aware of the many advantages he had in many aspects of training.

Three females and one male, against all the odds. Add on top of that we're seventeen, which the Earth Linx must be as well. This all seems like a joke. A very sick joke.

"Viv – Viv!" Zoe was impatient for my attention.

"Sorry, did you say something?" I quickly replied.

"No, but you looked a bit lost. I was starting to believe you were going to slip away from us again. I'm not sure if you realize it or not, but you're useless to the cause when you're dormant."

Ollin let out a bit of a laugh, but I knew the words she spoke were true. I needed to do my best to remain present. We needed to unravel as much as we could. Facing Tecuciztecatl and his legion would not be easy. Not in the slightest. Preparation was of the utmost urgency.

"I'm good. Just considering everything we know, that we need to prepare for. Training for one, especially mastering our weapons." Letting out a sigh I continued. "We have no idea what our enemies strengths and weaknesses are. For crying out loud, we don't even know who exactly were fighting. Sure we have a prophecy, filled with riddles. But it's up to us to unravel it, and the Calpulli can only help us so much."

Turning towards the window, praying nothing would be staring back at me, I continued. "I fear so much of the unknown, but if the fate of the human race rests on our shoulders, I will not go down without a fight." I walked toward the window as I added, "We need to locate the fourth Linx, and quickly.."

The room remained silent for awhile, as we contemplated a plan. None of us dared to speak as if doing so would hinder our thought processes.

I could feel their energies, as my own grumbled from deep within. Reflecting back on Alasdair and Coyolxa, the incident of just a few hours earlier. It didn't seem as if she was on the property, at least not physically. But her powers were strong enough to wreak havoc. *Are our powers as strong as hers? This will have to be tested,* I told myself.

Ollin stood up, reminding us of our original goal of the night; to discern the whereabouts of the fourth Linx. Without a word, Zoe hopped into action and Ollin and I followed.

As the guest house came into view, we could see that most of the downstairs lights were on, and it appeared the men were all still up; some seated at the kitchen island and others in the kitchen. They seemed to be working something out, well that was until they noticed our arrival. Mia was there, staring right at me through the window. She barked happily, alerting them to our presence.

I was a bit disappointed to lose the opportunity to eavesdrop, but Zoe was more optimistic. "It's better that we're up front with them going forth anyway."

I agreed with her, and so did Ollin.

The front door swung wide, and Jim our driver quickly ushered us in. "How are you Viv?" he inquired and once he was convinced I was fine, we joined the others in the open space.

"Shouldn't you all be sleeping?" Mr. Anderson asked sternly.

Before Zoe had a chance to reply, Ollin and I quickly jumped in. We knew Zoe would make matters worse because of her relationship with her father.

"We couldn't sleep, "Ollin and I both said at once. Everyone chuckled at that.

"Really, for you all to expect us to be able to sleep under the circumstances is pretty funny," Ollin added.

I went on to explain how we felt they were keeping information from us, including information regarding the Earth Linx. I purposely left out what Zoe had heard. It wasn't the time to add fuel to the fire between her and her father.

"In addition," I wanted to set the record straight, "We're the ones who are supposed to head this charge. You all need to stop treating us like children. No more secrecy."

CHAPTER TWENTY

The fall air felt crisp and cool as we pulled into the circular driveway in front of Kentwood High. Unlike the Catholic girl's boarding school I'd just come from, this one was swarming with teenage boys and girls scattered everywhere, and parents dropping them off. A row of school buses slowly approached from behind, so my father instructed Jim to find a visitor parking spot to wait in. Zoe and I got out, as Ollin, Alasdair, and Mr. Anderson exited the car behind us.

Ollin, of course, had wanted to arrive in his brother's McLaren, but the adults all agreed he could save the showing off for another day. Today was about matriculating.

Taking a deep breath, we followed our fathers

along the sidewalk. Humberto caught up to us as we were entering the building. I wasn't sure why he needed to come along, but he was there. As if we needed a larger entourage.

So much for making an inconspicuous entry. We stuck out like sore thumbs, and it seemed that all eyes were upon us, the new kids. I hadn't been the new kid since grade one, heck, neither had Zoe. This was definitely a first for us.

Our large group made its way through the front doors into a hallway where some staff members were mingling, and a security guard was speaking to a very tall bald man. The bald guy terminated his conversation immediately and approached our group with a broad smile.

"Good morning to you all! How can I help you? My name is Mr. Statefield, and I am the principal here at Kentwood."

My father took over the introductions, and the explaining, while Zoe, Ollin, and I looked around, and at each other.

Soon we were in the office getting registered. That's when I remembered Alasdair would be joining us. No wonder he had a terrified expression. I smiled at the thought.

A few moments later a secretary walked over to join our gathering. Humberto handed her what I guessed were transcripts, and to my surprise, guardianship papers. It turned out he was Ollin and Alasdair's guardian.

I rummaged through my memory trying to recall when their father had passed. Sure enough, it all started coming together. That must have been why he'd gone incommunicado for the past two years. It still didn't excuse his absence when my mother was ill or missing her funeral.

"So three of you are juniors and you Alasdair are a senior. How nice." Said the secretary. "We should have your schedules set up in no time at all. All hands on deck." She joked as she walked away with the documents in hand.

While Mr. Statefield conversed with our fathers and Humberto, a student helper was assigned to give us a quick tour of the school, while we waited for our schedules to be printed.

The school was a typical large high school. The school mascot was a Conqueror, yes the type that wears full armor and rides a horse, wielding a shield and sword. Black, green and silver seemed to be the school colors.

The cafeteria was immediately outside the office, as were all of the other administrative offices such as counselors and attendance, as well as the library. As we walked towards the gym the hallways were empty, classes having already started.

The student helper was a small Asian girl who was quite bubbly and very talkative. We arrived at a gym, which she explained was only one of two, and pointed in the direction of the other. We exited the school so she could point out a separate building where we'd most likely be having classes, and also pointed out some portables, a tennis court and a greenhouse behind the second gym.

As we walked back toward the main entrance, she pointed to our right. "That's the seniors parking lot, and that's the performing arts center, also known as PAC." Then we walked back through the front doors and into the office, rejoining the others.

Mr. Statefield thanked the girl who just smiled and headed to own her class. "You'll all know where everything is in no time. I'm not sure how well our school will compare with your previous ones, but we will do our best to make you feel at home," he assured us.

Zoe mumbled something under her breath, no doubt having to do with the school comparison.

Just then the secretary bustled up with our schedules in hand. She assured us that if we needed to make any changes, the counselors would do their best to accommodate our requests.

The four of us scanned the pieces of paper we'd been handed.

I had Spanish 3, AP Calc, AP Government, Science, and English. With the exception of the two AP classes, it seemed rather straightforward.

Zoe quickly looked over to compare her schedule with my own, noting we had three classes together; Spanish, Science, and English. Ollin had no classes with us, except the same lunch period.

Ollin grabbed Alasdair's schedule to compare with

ours. As it turned out, I had AP Government with him, and he had the same lunch as us.

Dad and the others were on their feet thanking the principal when Jim appeared with our backpacks. He must've picked them up when he left the Lummi reservation, as they were full of supplies.

Zoe rolled her eyes, and I gave her a nasty look for doing that to Jim.

"Thank you, Jim. These are great!" I said as I gave him a hug. Ollin and Alasdair thanked him as well. Zoe was left with no choice but to join in grudgingly.

Jim ignored her. He'd witnessed an outburst or two between Zoe and her driver in the past.

"Well kids, you're on your own," Humberto said, talking low, as we walked out of the office. "No assignments today. Today is for the four of you to get a feel for the school. Make yourselves familiar with the layout. Alasdair has a mapping device in his backpack. He's familiar with the technology and will start mapping the school when he can do so discreetly." He looked at Alasdair who simply nodded. "Enjoy your first day at your new school, and don't be afraid to make friends. It will be good for you to fit in."

Our fathers said their farewells quickly, as another student helper urged us to get a move on so we could reach our second-period classes in time. She showed us to our classes in closest order. My AP Calc class was in the detached building behind the gym, so she dropped me off last, giving the teacher a quiet introduction of who I was before she left.

I stood there awkwardly, as the entire class stared. Mr. McGraw was a youngish teacher and seemed pretty hip. "OK, listen up everyone, this is our newest student, Viviana Villareal. Why don't you tell the class a little about yourself, Viviana? I trust the other students will introduce themselves to you during breaks."

I couldn't think of much to say that was of any importance so I just said. "Thank you, Mr. McGraw. Hello, everyone. I played soccer at my last school and also play...ed competitively with a girls soccer club. I enjoy movies and travel whenever I get the chance, and spending time with my family. I like to read bestsellers, especially fantasy. I look forward to getting to know many of you in the weeks ahead." I could feel my face burning with embarrassment as I took my assigned seat. Each time I looked around, I'd catch someone staring at me. My stomach was in knots.

I hesitated when I mentioned the soccer club as I suddenly realized I didn't know whether I would still be able to participate in that part of my life anymore. *How much will this 'humanity saving' business cut into my lifestyle?* I wondered.

It wasn't long before the next bell rang. I quickly grabbed my map and set off to look for my AP Gov class. At least there I'd have company. Mr. McGraw asked if I needed any assistance, but it seemed fairly simple from what I could see on the map.

As I joined the throng of students in the hallway, the path ahead of me just kept opening as the students moved to let me through, I was sure not out of kindness, but mostly for a chance to stare at me. I was wondering if the others were experiencing the same thing.

When I arrived at my AP Gov class, Alasdair was already there. The room was filling up as the teacher held us both up front to do a proper introduction and seat assignment.

When she realized we knew each other, she inquired as to our relationship. Alasdair did me the honors of covering this.

"My father passed away two years ago. Viviana's uncle became guardian to my brother and I. We recently moved to this area as he and Viviana's father are starting a new venture together." He kept a straight face throughout.

"Oh! I'm truly sorry to hear that. So very sorry. If you need anything, just let me know. I'm here as an educator to support you through the remainder of your high school career."

On that note, the bell rang, and once again we became the object of many stares and hushed conversations. This time was different, though, the gals were outwardly eyeing Alasdair, while the guys were sizing him up as a potential rival. Well, not all of them. It was pretty obvious who the players were in that class.

It was nice not being the only new one in class, and I had to give Alasdair credit, he handled it all like a champ.

I wasn't sure if the seating plan was intended to be

sexist, but the teacher seated me among the few gals in the class. It was a male-dominated room, which was fine. But coming from an all-girls school, it was a little intimidating.

A few of the guy's fist bumped Alasdair as he made his way to his seat. I, on the other hand, was met with mostly cold stares.

Once I was in my seat, I noticed a less than attractive guy flashing his best attempt at a killer smile at me. I was unsure of the best way to respond, but just then a chuckle came from over my shoulder, so I immediately turned to see who it was. The girl was pretty in her own way, but as our eyes connected, I could sense her disapproval of me. I simply shook my head and refocused my attention on the front of the class. I'd make sure to return the smile to the well-meaning classmate, later.

As we made our way to the lunch room, I noticed Jim standing just inside the main doors. Both Alasdair and I made our way over to him.

"Hey! What are you doing here?" I inquired, as he swung a drawstring sack around. "Lunches. Sorry, we forgot about them until we arrived back at the house and the chef had them sitting on the kitchen island." I hadn't even thought about eating until now, but I was excited to find out what Gustav had prepared for us.

"Thank you, sir," Alasdair remarked kindly. Jim simply winked in our direction as he made his way out.

Ollin and Zoe found us as we searched for an empty table. The noise level was high in the cafeteria, but while there were still many stares directed at us, it wasn't as bad as when we'd been alone.

We soon found an empty table in the center of the room and quickly seated ourselves in such a way as to discourage anyone else from joining us.

Opening our brown paper bags, which was a first for me, we discovered each lunch had been meticulously matched to our individual tastes. A hearty salad for me, accompanied by sea salt caramel popcorn, a water bottle, and a package of gum. Alasdair and Ollin each had hearty artisan sandwiches, while Zoe's was a fruit mixture.

We attempted to make small talk, but the noise level was too high. I scooted over closer to Zoe which was a mistake. A couple of gals approached our table, eager to talk with Ollin, while clearly eyeing Alasdair.

I wasn't sure why that should bother me, but as I turned to speak to Zoe, I discovered she was equally perturbed by the uninvited guests.

Zoe asked how my morning classes had gone, but I couldn't seem to focus on replying to her, as I was trying to eavesdrop on the conversation that was taking place across from us. The blatant flirting was comical. The guys, of course, were soaking up all of the attention. I'm sure it was very flattering to their egos.

"Gee I wish they'd leave already. I'm really curious about the gadget they gave Alasdair to map the school. I also want to know what else he knows. He probably knows where the secret entrance is to our training facility by now," Zoe added between mouthfuls of fruit.

"Exactly! I'm dying to know as well." I had actually forgotten all about it, but I didn't want her to know that.

Ollin piped up, "I'm going to be attending a home football game this Friday, and they're looking for volunteers to help organize homecoming." Zoe rolled her eyes. She obviously could care less about football. I, however, was extremely bothered.

"How on earth can you be thinking about football games and homecoming? We have a mission, don't lose sight of that," I blurted out.

They all stared at me. Alasdair spoke up at that moment, "Viv, don't forget where you are. You need to keep calm." I started to challenge him, but he just continued, "Be very careful. Your eyes might give you away, and nobody else here will understand what's going on."

I stormed off, tugging out my map. I quickly realized I was headed in the wrong direction, but I didn't care. I charged forth. Surely there would be some leniency for a new girl on her first day. I wasn't giving anyone the satisfaction of witnessing my mistake.

Strolling the hallways, I gradually calmed down. In the state I was in I hadn't even noticed when the halls had cleared or heard the bell that precipitated the clearing.

I took a deep breath, and refocused on my whereabouts, eventually finding my way to my next class. Before entering the classroom, I dragged my fingers through my hair to tidy it up a bit.

The same lame introductions took place yet again, and as I was shown to my seat, I passed Zoe. Darn it! I'd completely forgotten she was in my last two classes. A tiny smile formed at the edges of her lips. No, it wasn't a polite, I'm happy to see you smile, but rather somewhat mocking.

The walk to our last class was rather subdued. This time the teacher allowed us to sit next to each other. As in the previous class, I sat staring straight ahead. Nothing seemed to be registering. Zoe, on the other hand, was busily taking notes. Typical of her, a high honors student with a perfect GPA.

The last bell brought a huge sense of relief. I urged Zoe to move faster, I needed to put distance between the school and me. It hadn't been a particularly good day.

As we walked toward the exit, a group of girls caught up to us. I recognized one of them from lunch.

"Hey! Wait." Someone exclaimed. I had planned on ignoring them, but Zoe stopped, kind of forcing me to do the same. Of all days to be engaging, why did she have to pick today?

"So you two are like, relatives of Ollin and Alasdair, right? Will you convince them to come out to our next home game?"

Really?! This is what they stopped us for?

"No, we're not relatives. Our families are just close friends." Zoe clarified. I had no idea why she even bothered.

"Oh!" The elected spokesperson said, sounding a bit disappointed.

Zoe leaned in as if to share some colossal secret. "Don't worry, as far as we know they're both single." She teased. It was enough to send the group into peals of laughter. But you just knew what they were all thinking. *Oh good, both guys are fair game.* The girls' obvious infatuation with the guys made me sick. I turned to escape only to run straight into a security officer. This was another huge difference from my previous school. Oh, we'd had security, but their presence was much more low key.

"Pardon me," I offered as I readjusted my backpack.

"Rough first day?"

Cinching the strap, I nodded in agreement.

"Are you a parent pick up, bus rider, or a walker?"

My expression must've given away my momentary confusion.

"Mode of transportation home?" He smiled softly.

Oh! Yes of course. "Parent pick up."

"You'll want to head over that way." He pointed behind the gym.

I thanked him and waited for Zoe to catch up. She tried to fill me in on the rest of the conversation, but I assured her I was not interested. As we reached the row of vehicles, I spotted the Audi at once and made my way towards it with Zoe close behind. I jumped in the front passenger seat, so Zoe climbed in the back.

We exchanged a brief greeting with Jim. But he

must've sensed our mood, and remained quiet after that.

As the cars crept slowly forward, we were finally at the curb nearest the gym, waiting for Ollin and Alasdair. They soon arrived, and we were on our way. Zoe filled them in about her conversation with the soccer players. It soon became clear that the game these gals had spoken of was the same football game Ollin already planned to attend. I'd completely forgotten how everywhere else in the world, soccer was football. I managed to tune out the rest of the talk.

When we arrived at the house, I jumped out of the car quickly, pushed my way through the front door, and went straight up to my room, locking the door behind me.

I rushed into my bathroom to splash cold water on my face. I needed to pull it together. My mood was absolutely atrocious, and I didn't really have a good reason.

Staring at the girl in the mirror, it was pretty apparent I'd lost some weight. Dark circles around my eyes, and 'oh my gosh' are those worry lines?

At that moment, I knew I needed to get a grip on myself. It was important for the Linx to work together as a cohesive team. I needed to embrace our new life. Sure, I didn't really have a choice. The lives of many innocents were our... my responsibility.

I never thought I could ever be this strong. Especially not after losing my mom. I now made up my mind to channel my love for her and use it as my reason to fight. I was now suspicious of the reason for her death. How much of it was organic, and how much was caused by unforeseen forces? That was something I had to find out for myself.

A knock at the door interrupted my thinking. I stood for a few moments longer, looking one more time at the girl in the mirror. It was time to reconnect.

"Alasdair? What are you doing here?" I felt butterflies in my stomach when I opened my door to find him standing on the other side. His lips moved, but nothing came out. I was taken aback.

"I just wanted to check in on you. Are you OK?" He finally blurted out.

I laughed, "Yes. Yes, I'm fine. I just wasn't ready for so many changes in one day. I suppose I was being a little petty. But I'm OK now."

He smiled, as his body relaxed. "Well, we're about to have a snack. Care to join us?"

I nodded, "I'll be along in just a few minutes." I closed the door and ran to my closet to change. Thankfully, someone had been thoughtful enough to transfer some of my clothes. I'd have to find out who that was and thank them properly.

As we chatted over milk and cookies, we told each other about our first day in the new school. It was nice to have typical teenage conversations again.

Ollin and Alasdair would be going to the girl's soccer game. We were invited, but Zoe and I both declined.

The adults were nowhere to be found, but Gustav

informed us that they hadn't returned since leaving that morning. We all sat quietly, trying to figure out what that meant.

Zoe and I decided to take a stroll around the stables. "You know," she said, as we admired the horses, "we desperately need to go shopping." I had to agree with her. We were in bad need of some new clothes.

"Weren't those girls hilarious," she said, "mooning over Alasdair and Ollin like that?" We both turned toward the sound of a galloping horse approaching across the backfield. Citlalli. I'd almost forgotten about her. Our last encounter was during her face off with Micteca. There was something about her riding style, and how her riding gear fit her, that reminded me of my mother. Another small tug at my heart strings.

"Hello, ladies. How are you today?" She asked as she dismounted beside us, and joined us on the cinder path.

We told her about our day, and Zoe told her about our decision to have a shopping expedition. Smiling, Citlalli invited herself along for the event. "I haven't been shopping in a very long time," she said. I didn't doubt that for a moment.

One of the stable hands came out to take the horse. Citlalli and Zoe discussed the different places we might go shopping, and after hearing the options, Citlalli said she'd organize the day. "Why don't the two of you keep Saturday open? We'll have to get an early start, though, so make sure you're up and ready bright and early and leave your gloomy selves at home. We're gonna be all about having fun." Something about her speech tickled our funny bones, so we all joined in the laughter. This is how my father found us, as he approached our laughing trio.

"I'm glad to see the three of you happy for a change." His words were sincere, especially so for me.

"I was just coming to get you all. We have some news, but it's best if we discuss it in private." The lightheartedness of the previous moment was gone, as we composed ourselves and followed him back to the main house. There, everyone gathered in the study again. Except that this time, there were two new people we'd never met before.

My father made the introductions. "Listen up everyone, I want you to meet Camilo and Xavier. They are fellow Calpulli and have been in direct contact with our comrades in Russia. They have some great news to tell you."

We all took seats and waited eagerly to hear what the newcomers had to say. Seeing our attentive faces, one of the men stood up to address us.

"Hello, everyone. I'm Camilo, and I'm very happy to inform you that our Earth Linx has been located. Actually, she wasn't all that hard to find, we simply followed up news reports of strange earthquakes and landslides in a remote area of the Ural Mountains in Russia."

"Her name is Natalie, she's 17 years old, and she's been an orphan since she was very young. Her parents left her well off, so she has spent most of her life in an old-fashioned boarding school. She is a classical dance prodigy but unfortunately has been unable to give public performances due to chronic shyness.

Three of our Calpulli brothers have been dispatched to bring her out before her culpability for the earthquakes can be proven. Fortunately, a contact of ours in that area of Russia realized what was going on and alerted us.

I found it interesting how they so easily mentioned another elemental as if we were just common folk.

"Another elemental? So what? There are whole herds of us just wandering the earth, waiting for each other to reveal our powers?" My question was legitimate, at least I thought so. But the look on Ollin and Zoe's face told me they understood this topic much better than I.

"As we've mentioned before, Viviana, there are certainly more elementals. But as powerful as the four of you? No." Humberto looked to Mr. Caberletti for confirmation.

"Yes, your uncle is correct. There are less than two-hundred in our ranks that we know of. If an elemental has very weak powers, the chances of us finding them are minimal. But for those like me, and the other members of the Calpulli present, we have a better way of detecting them." He smiled smugly. "Technology has helped. In the sense that we can follow strange weather patterns, or natural disasters, more conveniently."

Zoe glared at me. It was the expression she used when she wanted to push the conversation along.

"Good to know," was all I said.

The visitors thanked the rest of us, then took their leave. As my father saw them to the door, Zoe whispered in my ear to allow her to ask the questions. This irritated me somewhat, but I knew it was the best way for us to be on the same page, I could always demand an explanation from her later for things I didn't understand.

Gustav announced dinner was ready to be served in the dining room.

Ollin started to open his mouth, but Zoe gave him a look that could kill, and he dummied up.

I had to hide my face, to keep from laughing.

No sooner had my father rejoined us than Zoe was already posing the first question.

"Natalie. How much do we know about her?" Her eyes darted from person to person. "For starters, does she speak English?"

"She speaks English, apparently quite fluently, thanks to being in an excellent boarding school. Her parents left her a substantial trust fund which ensured she'd want for nothing. Well, at least anything money could buy." Uncle Humberto added with a grim smile.

The questions continued, mostly from Zoe as the rest of us sat back and let her go to it. When was she first detected? Two weeks ago. Had she been briefed? Yes. When will she arrive? In three days time. Most importantly, how is she taking it? The answer, not well at all, brought the room to silence.

I had a quick flashback of my own coming into my powers, and a shiver ran down my spine. I could only imagine what it must be like to learn this about yourself from a random stranger, and not have anyone by your side to love and support you.

I felt my mothers love all around me. Of course, I knew she was no longer here. The thought that I'd played along as if she'd never left my side made me cringe a little. Once again, I was so thankful to my father and my cousin Brian for being there for me.

Zoe and I had our fathers. Ollin and Alasdair had Uncle Humberto. I felt a tiny pang in my heart. Who would Natalie have?

I realized how lonely her life must have been, growing up. I glanced around taking a good look at our mismatched group. What about us made us so 'special' to have received these powers. Surely there had to be a common denominator. At that moment I knew I was onto something. I just didn't know what.

CHAPTER TWENTY-ONE

The uneventful morning had brought more stares and whispers among my fellow classmates, even in AP Gov, the class I shared with Alasdair. But now I was eager for lunch, wanting to learn more about the mapping device Alasdair had been carrying around, and of course anxious for more news of Natalie.

The chime finally rang and Alasdair, and I quickly found our way to the busy lunch room where we found Zoe and Ollin sitting at the same table. Maybe this would now be our table. The thought brought a smile to my face.

We were quizzing Alasdair about the device when we felt a shift in our surroundings. A very strange shift indeed. The light that had been pouring in through the windows dimmed drastically as dark clouds moved in. No one else in the room seemed to notice, but the four of us went on high alert.

I was about to ask Alasdair how the mapping of the school was going when a high pitch shriek split the air. Clapping my hands over my ears, I winced in pain and dropped to my knees. My element attempted to break through, but I knew I had to do everything in my power to contain it. It would be extremely dangerous to reveal myself in front of so many, so I concentrated harder.

A hand was on my back, I recognized Alasdair's energy. Unlike Zoe's and Ollin's, his energy was electrifying. He was sending small currents through my skin with enough voltage to release the tension in my head, or at least enough to distract me. Moments later the shrieking stopped, and the room was once more flooded with natural light. I returned to my seat with trepidation. Who might have witnessed me in terrified confusion?

To my surprise, it didn't appear that many had. One couple stared awkwardly in our direction, but there didn't seem to be any move to check more closely. Zoe and Ollin studied me out of the corners of their eyes, as they continued to make small talk, attempting to downplay the incident. It seemed to be working.

Alasdair didn't bother to conceal his concern. He stared at me intently, as if waiting for something to happen. I suppose at that moment, it had been customary for me to pass out. But not this time. Maybe

I was finally starting to adjust. After all, I'd easily contained my element. Sure Alasdair had helped, but I was sure I could have done fine without him.

I offered him a reassuring smile. I was OK. At least for the moment.

"So, Natalie?" I broke the silence. I knew trying to figure out what Alasdair was thinking was dangerous. I wasn't ready to go down that road.

"What about her?" Ollin countered.

"You're kidding, right? Are we supposed to ignore that she'll be here in a couple of days?" Zoe challenged him.

"No," Alasdair said firmly, "No. We're not supposed to do anything. The Calpulli shared all they could with us. It's for our own safety." He took a deep breath. "Listen to me very carefully Zoe. You need to pay attention to the Calpulli's instructions. Deviating is not an option. It could be very dangerous." He focused more on Zoe than anyone else. She glared furiously back at him. The level of energy coming off of her was alarming, but Alasdair didn't back down.

Ollin broke the standoff. "Look bro. I get it. We get it. But on the same note, what are we supposed to do when we know they're not being forthright with us?"

My thoughts wandered back to a time I wouldn't have minded getting lost in right then. Tadeo was once more on my mind. Alasdair had planted the seed, by emphasizing our safety. I remembered what Vitale had revealed about his shot at fulfilling the prophecy. Did

Alasdair know about that? Was this why he was cautioning us? I couldn't bring it up without revealing what I'd been experiencing during my dream travels.

* * *

Science class was as uneventful as ever. However, it turned out one of the girls from the soccer team was in our English class. She cornered Zoe immediately as we entered the classroom. I purposely avoided her by going directly to my seat but noticed she and Zoe looking at me as they chatted.

"What was that all about?" I questioned Zoe, as soon as I knew no one could overhear our conversation.

"They heard that you play soccer, and were hoping I could convince you to play in a pickup game over the weekend. Personally, I think it's just a ploy to get closer to Ollin and Alasdair. Anyway, I told her I'd mention it to you, but not to hold her breath."

"Good." Was all I'd replied.

I'd had to quit my school team when I changed schools and hadn't given them a second thought since. Zoe had quit the swim team as well. *What else were we giving up? Oh, that's right, possibly our lives*, I thought to myself sarcastically. The dangers, however, were real. I knew this first hand since I'd already encountered two of Tecuciztecatl's demon goddesses in person.

Vitale had been correct, we couldn't afford any distractions. I looked around the classroom, stroking my hair absentmindedly. Every single person in that room, in that school, in that community, had no idea of the danger they were in. A twinge of guilt came over me as I thought about how our very presence at this school placed them in harm's way.

At the end of the day, it wasn't Jim who picked us up. It was Citlali. I could sense her calming influence as we got in the car. Something was up.

"Everything OK?" I asked.

"Yes." She smiled sheepishly. I could tell she was lying.

"Where's Jim?" I pressed her for more information.

"He was sent on an errand. He and Gustav won't be back until tomorrow, and the rest of the Calpulli are currently occupied." She informed us as she drove out of parking lot. But she didn't head toward the house. Taking a different exit than usual from the Foss Roundabout, she headed straight to the library and pulled into the parking lot.

Naturally, we immediately questioned what we were doing there. She shrugged, "Orders are for you all to do your homework here while I review the data in the mapping device with Alasdair."

The mapping device did exactly that, map the school. There was a preloaded blueprint of the school on the device, but Alasdair with the device in hand was tracking exact distances and unforeseen obstacles. Once he'd gone through the entire school, a file would be created and loaded via an app to our phones. This would help us track each other should the need arise.

Citlali had other things on her mind. I tried to press her for more information, but it was useless.

Once we were done, she drove us to a local burger

joint. The dinner rush had just started as we placed our orders. Alasdair was leaning across the table in conversation with Citlali. I wouldn't have cared, except I could feel her eyes on me.

"Now what?" I muttered to myself.

Citlali sounded serious when she turned to me. "Tell me what you experienced in the cafeteria?"

I'd almost forgotten the incident. She knew I couldn't lie to her.

"I felt the same as I did the other night back at the house, only this time Alasdair was able to help me get through it much more calmly."

I would've rubbed my face but remembered just in time I was wearing a little mascara, so I settled for stroking my hair instead.

"You felt or you heard? These details are important Viviana."

I nodded my head in understanding. "I heard the high pitch screech, but I also felt a shift in the energy. I think we all did." I looked to the others for reassurance. They all nodded in agreement.

Citlali studied me a few more moments, well at least till the waitress interrupted with our tower of onion rings. I was suddenly no longer hungry, but I grabbed one anyway.

Our dinner went quietly, as did our drive back to the house. When we arrived, we found the house empty.

"Where is everyone?" Zoe asked as she tossed her backpack onto the floor.

I noticed both Alasdair and Ollin surveying the house carefully. I attempted to listen or even feel for something, but nothing came. I wondered what they were picking up on if anything.

"Don't waste your time, you two. There's nothing here." Citlali eyed them, before turning to me, probably knowing I too was trying to pick up on whatever Alasdair and Ollin were doing.

"I've already told you they've gone to attend to some things. The three of you, go grab your weapons from the library. Alasdair, you get yours too."

Zoe and I looked at each other. What weapon did Alasdair posses? The only other weapon in the bundle belonged to Natalie.

"All of you meet me at the stables." She instructed as she walked out of the house.

Zoe and I followed Ollin into the library. He laid the large leather bag on the floor and flipped it open. I marveled once more at how beautiful these fighting instruments were.

"What weapon does your brother possess?" Zoe asked as she gathered up her daggers. The daggers really suited her. Ollin attached his satchel to his belt loop as he answered. "You'll see." He chuckled.

We made our way out to the stables, Zoe still obviously irritated with Ollin for not telling her what she wanted to know. She pulled up short with a startled squeal as she almost ran into Alasdair who just seemed to materialize out of thin air. We'd been completely distracted, and I realized this was something we would have to work on. We would have to become more aware of our surroundings.

Alasdair said nothing, as he adjusted a black strap that fit tightly across his chest. When he turned to face us, the haft of a sword came into full view. It was plain and simple, shaped like a silver cross. The handgrip was tightly wrapped in strips of leather. I reflected upon this briefly, because I knew this type of sword wasn't part of the Aztec weaponry.

Citlali wasn't actually in any of the stables, we found her in the indoor training arena. She'd changed into her leathers, and beside her on the ground was an open black leather bag. The weapons within the bag were similar to our own, except where ours were adorned in black, hers were in jade.

"I guess we missed the memo to change clothes?" I made a stab at humor. I was more than a tad jealous of how gorgeous and lethal Citlali looked.

"You will each be fitted for gear once Natalie arrives. By the way, she'll be arriving much sooner than we had anticipated. It seems there was a minor setback, but the Calpulli has it under control." A mischievous smile played around her lips, as she reached for her sword.

In a single sweep, she'd raised the sword and swung it towards Alasdair.

In a panicked surprise, the rest of us jumped back, but Alasdair was ready. He'd somehow anticipated her move and fended off her attack easily with his own weapon. Amused, she stepped back but only to fully engage him. He'd been ready and accepted the challenge.

The ensuing battle was very intense, neither seemed to be holding back. I was quite impressed with how well Alasdair handled himself and his sword, but Citlali was intriguing to watch. Her manipulation of the weapon seemed effortless, as the clash of metal on metal resounded throughout the arena. It wasn't long before Alasdair started to breathe heavily and perspire, whereas Citlali was totally unphased, almost mocking him at each thrust and parry. He held her off a bit longer, but it was obvious he was growing tired as he shifted into more of a defensive mode rather than attacking and counterattacking. They continued for a few more moments, and then Citlali lowered her sword and backed away.

She walked back to her bag, swapping the sword for the smaller twin blades. For a brief moment, Zoe's expression showed terror, but she quickly recovered herself and moved into position facing Citlali.

"While I instruct Zoe, everyone listen up, because it applies to all of you," Citlali said.

She spoke at length about foot placement, awareness of surroundings, and many of the positions specific to protecting oneself during an attack. She then switched up for Ollin, grabbing her version of his weapon. She shifted to instructing us on how to properly hold our weapons, discussing the muscle groups that we would be using when handling them, and the best methods for building those muscles.

Without a word, she once again switched weapons. It was now my turn.

As I clutched my spear, the lights of the arena grew dim. Apparently, Citlali had asked Ollin to turn them down. "All of your fights will occur at night." Citlali cautioned, "Tecuciztecatl is after all the Moon God, and he is most powerful during that time."

"Everything that's been happening is meant to unnerve you all, especially you Viviana."

I could feel the eyes of the other on me.

"It's time to share with your friends what's been going on Viviana. Remember, this information is not to be spoken of outside this group. Well, except for Natalie of course." I looked at her in confusion. What was she talking about?

"Viviana has been traveling back to Aztec civilization in a dream state known as Yalhua . It's a bit more symbolic than that. But the three of you need to understand this, the Four Gods will communicate with you via Viviana."

They were all looking puzzled at this revelation.

"There is one more thing you should be aware of. There was an earlier failed attempt to fulfill this prophecy." She slowly turned back to me. "Three of the original Linx are still stuck there in that time and place."

"Wait – original Linx?" Zoe blurted out.

"Yes. The original Linx failed their mission fifty years ago." Citlali offered.

"What happened to the fourth?" It was Ollin who

quizzed her this time. I noticed Alasdair studying me carefully, giving me the feeling he felt I'd been betraying them.

"He's dead." I knew I sounded a bit callous. "He died when one of the Linx deviated during an attack. Which is why it's important that we all stick to the plan. Dysfunction brings on chaos, and that's what these evil deities are waiting for." I took in a deep breath. "They expect us to fall apart and they expect infighting." Alasdair continued watching me as I spoke.

"Yes, Viviana is exactly right." I was wondering if Citlali was going to reveal her true identity, but she didn't. Instead, she brought the conversation back to training. This time she engaged me, as she had Alasdair. Only with not quite as much intensity.

Ollin and Zoe directed me as I fumbled with my spear. It wasn't easy getting used to maneuvering the long handle. I was soon sweating, profusely, but Citlali showed no signs of stopping.

"Let your instincts take control," Alasdair said. I'd almost lost control at the sound of his words. It was the exact same thing Vitale had said to me. Although I was rapidly becoming exhausted, I fought on.

For a brief moment, I remembered how I'd read Vitale' weakness. How he'd favored one side and protected his ribs. Then I remembered feeling ridiculous when Tadeo took me to train with the others. I strengthened my resolve and began a counter-attack.

My spear was still being a bit of a challenge, but I fought on with determination. Citlali pushed back, a bit harder, causing me to stagger.

"Find her weaknesses," Alasdair exclaimed excitedly. *Yes, I know. I'm trying.* But something was off somehow. I couldn't concentrate on what he was saying. It felt like Deja Vu.

"Focus!" He yelled. This time I caught a glimpse of what I'd been searching for. At that moment I could actually see Alasdair, the real Alasdair. He was truly in his element.

Once more, I engaged Citlali, fighting back with all my strength. *Krav Maga*, I thought, and though I wasn't entirely inexperienced, I was still no match for Citlali. I pushed on, just as I'd pushed when training in the Aztec realm. Then, as I fought on fiercely, something began to feel familiar. His energy. There was something about Alasdair's energy that I'd found myself vaguely attracted to, and just like that it all came to me in a rush.

Stopping in my tracks, I turned to face Alasdair. Citlali must've done the math in her head, as she quietly lowered her weapon and stepped back.

"You. You're him, aren't you?" Zoe and Ollin stared at me in even more confusion than they had when Citlali revealed the truth about my dream traveling.

I circled him slowly, ready to pounce if he didn't answer truthfully. He remained stock still. I wasn't sure if it was because he was afraid of me or had merely decided to let this play out.

"So what? You're just going to stand there? Tell me!" I yelled. I'd promised myself earlier that I'd work at controlling myself, but by now my element had found it's way out. I stood there holding a ball of flame in my free hand.

A gasp came from behind me, and when I looked around, Zoe was pointing at my spear. The metal was glowing red from the heat my element was generating. Ollin had taken a defensive stance, his eyes already revealing the power of his element.

"What do you want to know Viviana?" His voice was calm. Too calm. What did he take me for, a fool?

The blue flames flickered around my body. Everyone except Citlali moved back even farther.

"That's enough Viviana," Citlali said soothingly. But my anger took control of me at the thought of her trying to manipulate my emotions. My hand raised of its own volition shooting flame in her general direction. It wasn't intended to strike her but to serve as a warning to leave me alone. She didn't even blink. I could tell she was trying hard to get inside my head, but my fury was great, and I pushed her out.

Alasdair moved into my peripheral vision, but Citlali waved him off.

"I said that's enough!" This time her voice was more menacing.

"Or what? What will you do?" I challenged her. She made one last attempt to get into my head, and again I shot flames in her direction, but this time it was dispersed by a water shield. I turned to Zoe fully expecting it had come from her. But it wasn't her, a quick glance at the others and nothing. I turned back to Citlali, whose eyes were like pools of ocean green.

"You forget that I am a goddess. Nahui Atl, Goddess of the Oceans." Her voice was dry, absent of emotion.

"The last time this earth was destroyed, it was I who destroyed it. Did you know this?" She continued. "Of course you didn't. That is because you are too young and naïve to care. I was the Fourth Sun, the Water Sun, Calchiuhtlicue. Stupidity and jealousy of the gods have always led to this earth's demise. Don't follow that path." Her voice trailed off.

I dropped to the ground, releasing my weapon, and quieting my element.

"I understand you are angry. It's natural to have these feelings. But you must not forget that fighting me, or any of your fellow Linx is not the answer. Don't feed the enemy." I caught her eyeing Alasdair.

I struck the ground with my fist and looked him in the eyes. "It's you, isn't it?"

There was no need for him to respond. I knew it was him. And he knew I knew. And Citlali knew.

"When were you planning on telling me?" My question was to both of them.

"Who is who?" Ollin asked in bewilderment. But we just ignored him.

"We didn't think you'd figure it out this soon. It was important to your training in the Aztec realm that this information be kept from you." She explained, "Mostly for the protection of the other three."

"What other three? What are you guy's talking about?" Now it was Zoe's turn to demand more information. I knew we couldn't keep this from them any longer.

"Alasdair is Isaiah," I said matter-of-factly, "Isaiah was the fourth original Linx, the one who died." I studied him carefully.

Saying it out loud seemed to make it all the more surreal. "I want to hear how this is possible," I finished.

Zoe and Ollin helped me up from the ground, as we waited for Alasdair to offer up an explanation. Alasdair looked toward Citlali who nodded assent.

He drove his fingers through his tangled locks, glancing around at us all then finally resting his gaze on Ollin.

"First, you must understand we truly are brothers." His eyes watered as he stared sympathetically at his brother. "I was reincarnated by the gods into this body. I died, yes, that much is true. I was reborn as Alasdair Radnitz, son of Marcus Radnitz, but I was formerly his own brother, Isaiah Radnitz."

We stood silently, letting his words soak in. Alasdair was his own father's brother reborn?

He continued. "I had been watching the waves breaking on the rocky shore. Coyolxa must have been scouting the area. I'm not sure how long she'd been observing me. I didn't even notice her there until I broke my reverie and was about to leave. At first, her presence startled me, but once I saw those burning red eyes, I was overcome with fear. I knew she was the enemy, and I needed to get away, but there seemed to be a disconnect between my feet and my brain. I stood there rooted to the spot, as she circled me slowly like a bird of prey.

That's when I first noticed my spark. It was so subtle I almost missed it. I blinked a couple of times thinking my terror was causing me to hallucinate, but the more I focused, the greater the rumble coming from my innards. My father reached us at that moment, but Coyolxa paid him no heed. For some reason, she was totally focused on me. Finally, Dad cast a furious blast of wind in her direction, barely missing me.

As I watched in astonishment Coyolxa's skin began to glow as if lighted from within. Strange symbols appeared, among which the moon was prominently featured, and tiny bells appeared on both of her cheeks. Each of the symbols on her skin began to glow and throb individually, causing strands of energy to flow towards her fingertips. As the energy accumulated in her hands, it formed into two pulsating golden orbs hovering over her palms.

I heard my father holler for me to run, but his words were interrupted by her counter attack. I snapped out of the trance I was in, fearing for my father. That's when I had the first flashback. An image of fighting with the three others. We appeared to be training, with our elements. The vision seemed to be prompting me to use the inner energy I held pent up within. When my father's face came back into focus, I didn't hesitate. Without mercy released a vicious attack on Coyolxa. Thunderous bolts of lightning scorched the shore and lit up the sky, missing her once, twice, three times, until finally, one penetrated the back of her right leg. Cowering, she retreated to the ocean, and disappeared right before our eyes."

The brilliance returned to Alasdair's eyes, as he summoned his energy source, just as any of the three of us would summon our elements. We stared in awe.

"Hurriedly, we found ourselves in a camouflaged room within the greenhouse I'd never seen before. Patting each of his pockets one by one, Dad finally located his cell phone tucked away in the inside pocket of his jacket. Visibly shaken by the incident, he started typing a message as another image invaded my mind. This time it was an actual fight. I wasn't exactly sure of the location, but I was moving stealthily down a residential street. Another person, about my age, was checking to see if the way was clear around the next corner. He motioned with his head for me to press forward, and as I did so, I caught a glimpse of my reflection in a window. I didn't recognize myself. Continuing the charge, we joined up with two other warriors who assured us the property was secured. At that moment my father snapped me back to the present. But the image of the reflection I'd seen was obviously Isaiah. My father's brother."

Alasdair was no longer giving off energy as he

finished his account. I could that Ollin was still in confusion. All any of us could do was listen. Not even the Calpulli seemed to understand how Alasdair and Isaiah were connected. What was the purpose? If he was here, and the others were in ancient Mesoamercia, then what was our true purpose? It was all so complicated.

The silence after Alasdair's last words was deafening. We all feel it deeply. This had all become a complicated riddle.

Finally, Citlali spoke, "The Creator's will reveal the purpose when it becomes necessary. In the meantime, you all must not allow yourselves to become distracted. As you now know, Alasdair is one of you. Viviana can dream travel, and will bring back skills with her to help you each learn the ancient art of warfare."

I words made me think again of The Shorn Ones. It was obvious they had no comprehension of Alasdair or Isaiah. How could this information be kept from them, and what was the true purpose?

CHAPTER TWENTY-TWO

We returned to the house exhausted, discouraged and confused. Very little was said after the revelation. Zoe and Ollin refused to make eye contact with me. So was Alasdair for that matter but I understood completely how they felt.

In the shower, my body welcomed the stinging hot spray, but I cut it short, anxious to get back to the others. I really needed to speak to my father and Humberto. The situation with Alasdair had me unsettled.

I dried hurriedly, then wrapped the towel around myself. I reached for another towel to dry my hair, but miscalculated the distance in my rush, slipped on the wet tiles and crashed onto the bathroom floor. My vision came in and out of focus as I slowly slipped into unconsciousness. The last thing I remembered was a sharp pain in my head.

* * *

It was still and dark as I slowly got to my feet. The air around me smelled musty. Searching for signs of life, I looked around dazedly focusing on a dim light in the distance which is when I noticed the rock walls. A cave? I was in a cave.

For a brief moment, I was tempted to go in the opposite direction, but the light beckoned to me. As if in a trance I stumbled towards it.

The floor rose steeply beneath me littered with rocks and debris. Soon I was perspiring profusely and panting hard. An uneasy feeling arose in the pit of my stomach, and for once it wasn't my element. Still, I reached deep within just to reassure myself it would be available if I needed it.

Abruptly the corridor widened out into a medium sized room, and the source of the light came into view causing me to stop and stare in wide-eyed amazement. A huge stone table sat in the center of the room and above the table hovered a mysterious glowing sphere. I approached cautiously. The sphere radiated phosphorescent blue light, and I could feel the energy coming from it.

Suddenly the sphere emitted a shrill blast like that of a factory whistle at quitting time, and I stumbled backward in surprise. Brief deafness ensued, followed by a blast of cold air that strangely struck me in my left hand.

For some strange reason my element had retreated, and my attempts to recall it were useless. Panicked, I scrambled back toward the corridor through which I'd come, but at that moment a heavy stone slab slid into place across the entrance with a thud, sealing me in the room with the frightening entity.

A crushing sense of fear suddenly overcame me, as the light source began to intensify. A few explicit words escaped my lips as a huge figure slowly materialized on the table top.

I hadn't noticed before how vast the space above me was, as the figure continued to expand upward into the shadows.

A deep, guttural laugh erupted from the being as he leered down at me.

I tried desperately to focus on my breathing, urgently trying to invoke my element again. A wave of terror washed over me as I tilted my head up and stared into those piercing eyes.

His derisive laughter echoed through the cavern.

His lower extremities remained obscured by the brightness of the light source, but I could see he was naked from the waist up. Lean and muscular, his eerie yet handsome features revealed a series of tattoos covering his shoulders and arms. A peculiar light was slowly tracing over the lines of his tattoos as if telling a story. My eyes followed the moving light, and strangely I understood the message. He turned his body slowly as the light moved across his torso and around to his back, upon which a massive full moon was tattooed. I inadvertently gasped at the sight as it slowly dawned on me who this being was.

As he grew larger, I had to keep backing up farther to keep him in sight. Suddenly I lost my footing and stumbled backward. As he turned his menacing glower on me something caused me to snap. At that moment my fear turned to anger, and I hissed at him viciously.

"Ocēlōtl," He boomed out in a roar that echoed throughout the cavern.

At that same instant, I bumped into something behind me and jumped around to see what it was only to discover it was the cavern wall. Looking down at the floor to be sure of my footing I was shocked to see two massive furry paws where my feet should have been.

Once more his bellow filled the cavern.

"The Jaguar Warrior. So, the prophecy is finally coming true."

A ferocious roar escaped my throat as I sent an enormous tongue of flames in his direction.

Snarling, I shouted back, "You, Tecuciztecatl, Moon God…creature of the night. You will fail."

Just as he moved to crush me, I rose, bouncing off the cavern wall and onto the table. My element flared hotly around me, casting off light that revealed an opening high on the far wall. My feline instincts propelled me toward that opening just as he made a grab for one of my hind legs, sending me crashing back down onto the table. *Aren't cats supposed to land on their feet?* I thought to myself as I dodged his massive fist?

Again, I worked my way back towards the opening. He hurled beams of light energy at me, and I did my best to dodge them. Again, I was unable to reach the opening.

My tail swished back and forth as I entered into the dance, the two of us trying to anticipate each other's next move.

His powers were strong, and I knew he could finish me anytime he chose. Why he had not done so by now was the real mystery. I decided whatever his plan was, he needed me to remain alive.

Once again, a flicker of blue sky through the opening caught my attention. In a split second, I leaped back on the table, launching myself from there with my powerful hind legs, causing the stone table to collapse from the force. This created enough of a distraction for me to reach the opening and claw my way out.

My long strides, urgent and powerful, carried me towards a wooded area.

The trees and overgrown vegetation provided cover for my flight, and the many noises of the night masked the sounds of my passage. I finally reached a pool of water where I paused to lap thirstily. The evening sky was still bright enough for me to see my reflection in the pool. And now, for the first time, I stared at the majestic creature I'd become.

I felt as much as heard footsteps behind me and retreated into the shadows of the trees. The fire returned to my eyes in anticipation as he came into view. Tadeo. I relaxed and sat back on my haunches, to await his arrival.

CHAPTER TWENTY-THREE

Magda's steady rhythm was now familiar to me, as I awoke in Tadeo's home. Staring up at the thatched roof, I wondered if it had all been a dream. My thoughts wandered back to the story that unfolded before me in his tattoos. I didn't fully understand everything, just enough to decipher his identity. The Moon God, Tecuciztecatl.

A sudden chill came over me as I remembered the struggle I'd had controlling my element during the encounter in the cave. Fear had prevented my element from manifesting while anger had caused it to flare up on its own. *My emotions are the key.*

The Jaguar Warrior he had called me. Ocēlōtl. Is that what I am?

My stomach finally got the better of me, so I wandered into the kitchen. Magda smiled and mumbled something I didn't understand. Her body language indicated I should take a stool, so I did so as she placed a bowl of food in front of me.

Once again, my nostrils filled with the inexplicably delicious aroma. A variety of colors stared back at me from the bowl of vibrant red stew, loaded with yellow squash and pinto beans.

She placed freshly made tortillas wrapped in a cloth to keep them warm, beside my bowl. The smell managed to filter through the cloth, penetrating my already overloaded olfactory senses.

I tore off a chunk of tortilla, topped it with meat and beans, and presented it to my taste buds. Absolutely delicious.

When I was finished eating, I wandered out the back door to find Tadeo busy expanding his dwelling. It didn't make a lot of sense to me since he was a single young man. I waved to him.

I wonder what Alasdair would be like if he too were stuck here, in this realm. Would he be the leader of The Shorn Ones?

Not far from the house I came upon a massive mescal plant. I knew a bit about the varieties, as my mother came from a family that made artisan mezcal. As I continued to stare, my thoughts wandered yet again to Alasdair. How alone he must have felt. His companions all here, he back there, separated from them.

I personally felt a link between myself and my two companions, so I figured it must be the same for him.

I wrapped my arms more firmly around myself, as a light breeze brushed against my skin. Sensing a presence behind me, I turned quickly on my heels and came face to face with Tadeo.

"How long have you been standing there?" I questioned.

"Not long." His gaze was unreadable. "How are you?"

"OK, I guess," I sighed, "Just when I believe I'm starting to understand something about the prophecy, something else comes up, and I'm right back to square one."

Carefully, he moved in closer. Perhaps sensing my apprehension, he stopped.

"Anything I can help you unravel?" He smiled.

Why did he smile? Why couldn't he just be his typical aloof self? Like a typical teenager, I stood there with butterflies in my stomach, upset with myself for allowing my feelings to have more control of me than they should have.

"All right. What do you remember about Isaiah?" A pang of regret suddenly overcame me. But, I was determined not to proceed further without transparency. I was done with trying to keep the two worlds apart. It was time to bring things together regardless of who may or may not approve. My life and the life of all the Linx were at stake, and that wasn't even counting the lives of the unsuspecting human race.

Somewhat taken aback, Tadeo opened and closed his mouth. Unsure of how to answer me, he stared at me instead, running his fingers through his wavy hair.

"Anything the matter?" I pressed, causing him to feel even more uneasy.

"I'm curious as to why you're suddenly asking about him now?"

Tadeo had no clue what I was about to reveal to him. For a moment, I gloated to myself. I had the upper hand on information, for once. He waited for me to reply but I just stood, silently staring him square in the face.

He struggled to regain his composure. Gradually the leader of The Shorn Ones returned.

A surge of energy reignited in me, as I stood defiantly. My element was at my fingertips, ready for my command. Except, I discovered I wasn't really all that eager to see Tadeo call upon his own element. I'd had suspicions that he and the other two were no longer able to call upon their elements. I was very wrong.

Tadeo's element was not like those of the other Linx. Once more I was faced with the same powerful electrical energy I'd come to recognize from Alasdair. What in the name of the gods was going on? Had their elements transformed?

CHAPTER TWENTY-FOUR

My entire being pulsated with the exhilaration of my element, ready to pounce on Tadeo. Something about him made me furious, and now, both of us were at the ready with our elements, and I would not back down.

I advanced on him, grinning at the confused expression on his face. Certainly, he didn't think me capable of sparring with him, especially not element to element. His capabilities carried years of refinement, whereas I was still a novice.

I cast flares at him, but they bounced harmlessly off his shield. A spark ignited in his eyes as he moved in closer, calculating my next move. An electromagnetic field was drawing me toward him, so I evaded it in a quick twisting motion. This time I discharged a huge burst of flame in an attempt to engulf him. Useless. His own energy simply consumed it. Somehow Tadeo was able to convert my element into his own personal energy source. His body glowed brightly, illuminating the surrounding landscape.

A combination of fear and desperation forced me to dislodge a firestorm at him as my element suddenly took on the blue fiery form I'd seen before. However, the slight moment of hesitation on my part had allowed Tadeo to counterattack, for which I was not prepared.

Soon, the crossfire between our elements grew in magnitude as gleams of his light source, and my blue fire swept the area around us, destroying everything they touched.

I stood incandescently, refusing to yield as my chest heaved in nervous anticipation of the attack I wouldn't be able to ward off.

Tadeo backed off several paces as if to allow me to gather my composure, but another burst of anger overcame me.

I released a thunderous growl, surprising even myself. My senses were heightened, and my resolve returned as I slowly circled around him. I let out a long hiss when he reached for his weapon.

His lips were moving, but I couldn't make out the words. My head was spinning as my enhanced senses picked up noises around me I had never been able to hear before. Yet I focused angrily on him.

Tadeo's face broke into a huge smile, "Jaguar Princess," he said.

I tried to ignore his words, but then I noticed he was beckoning me to follow him. With some reluctance, I followed as he led me across the road and down a small embankment to a pond. I looked at him in confusion, but he continued to point to the water. Finally, I realized he wanted me to look at my reflection.

My vestments were grand, transformed from those I'd worn in the past. The glowing light from my flames clearly revealed the jaguar markings on my skin. I gasped at what I'd become.

I was still confused. What on earth was happening to me? I turned back to Tadeo and could see he was truly captivated by what I had become.

"I'm not sure what is happening to me. What do you mean by Jaguar Princess?" My voice cracked.

"You, Viviana, are the strongest of all the Linx, of all the elementals who've ever roamed the earth. If I were to compare you to all the figures in Greek Mythology, you are above a demigod. There have been rumblings about a Linx possibly being able to transform, but there is nothing about it in the Codices. The Four never confirmed nor denied when I asked them that question. But now I understand why. They knew I would find out for myself." He looked at me with wonderment in his eyes.

I cautiously backed away from him, not sure if my transformation was a good thing or not. Whirling on the balls of my feet I ran towards the temple, carried swiftly by my new-found speed as the people I passed gazed in wonder. Surely, I had become a freak of nature.

I didn't hesitate upon my arrival, but rushed straight to the portal and burst through it. Once on the other side, I found myself on the floor of my bathroom, only remembering that I had fallen.

* * *

I sat on the edge of my bed, still wrapped a towel when I heard a quiet tap on the door.

"Who is it?" I said loud enough for the person on the other side to hear me.

"It's me, Zoe. Are you ready to go downstairs?"

A quick look at my clock confirmed that very little time had passed. I opened my door cautiously, beckoned Zoe to enter and eased the door shut with a soft click.

"Are you OK? You look super pale." Zoe spoke with genuine concern as she seated herself in an armchair by the window.

"I slipped and fell when I got out of the shower. I think I passed out." I offered, hoping it would ring true.

"Good grief, Viv! Are you okay?"

"I'm a little dazed. But I feel fine," I gathered my clothes and stepped into the bathroom leaving the door ajar so we could continue talking.

"Look, Zoe. I'm really sorry for not offering you more information on Yalhua. You know, the dream travel? I wasn't even sure it was real in the beginning, and I thought if I talked about it, you guys might think I was crazy. After all, I did go around believing my mother was still with me for quite a while." I waited for her reply, but instead, Zoe was pushing the bathroom door open.

"What is that?" She exclaimed, staring at my reflection in the mirror. I couldn't see very well, so she reached for a hand mirror I'd left on the counter earlier that morning when I'd made a weak attempt to apply makeup.

Zoe angled the mirror so I could get a glimpse of my back.

I stood there petrified. What on earth? I stared at tattoo like markings on my back resembling the sun with jaguar print as a backdrop. Tears fell from my eyes as I remained there, frozen in disbelief. What was happening to me? Zoe finally broke the silence.

"Stay here, I'm going to get Citlali," and she quickly disappeared.

I didn't move. I stood there shivering, holding my top against my chest. At least I'd had the opportunity to put on my underwear.

Zoe and Citlali entered my room, and Zoe secured the lock behind her as Citlali joined me in the bathroom. She said nothing, simply turned me around to look at my back. It seemed like forever before anyone spoke.

"Get dressed, we'll wait for you in the bedroom," Citlali said as she closed the bathroom door. More tears spilled down my cheeks as I dressed.

When I stepped out, I found Zoe sitting on my bed, propped against the headboard, and Citlali staring out the window. She turned to face me.

"Viviana, I need you to be completely honest with me. What happened to you in Yalhua?" her voice, insistent.

I explained everything in as much detail as I could remember, while she stood there, arms crossed. When I had nothing else to offer, she reached for a strand of her hair and wrapped it around her fingers, a nervous tendency which I shared.

Taking a deep breath, she sat on the edge of the armchair with her elbows on her knees, hands together and fingers entwined. Zoe and I waited patiently for her to say something, anything.

"So, Tadeo knows," she said slowly, but seemed like she was talking to herself, so I didn't answer.

She finally looked up at me, "You are very different from the other Linx. It's not real complicated, but I'm afraid I'm not at liberty to discuss it with you, at least not yet. If I do, we run the risk of the Four Gods removing me from this mission. That would be extremely risky. You all need me," her voice trailed off into silence once again. Zoe and I simply stayed where we were, waiting for her to continue, which she eventually did. "I assure you both I will share more as soon as I find it safe to do so. For now, we will keep this to ourselves, understand? In the meantime, we need to get downstairs, we have a special guest."

Zoe and I looked at each other, both of us wondering who it could be.

CHAPTER TWENTY-FIVE

When I arrived at the kitchen, Ollin was sitting with his back to me, engaged in conversation with someone. Then I noticed the tall, thin girl standing uneasily next to the kitchen island. She appeared to be very pale and delicate.

When I say, Ollin was conversing, it seemed to be entirely one-sided on his part. The girl remained silent, taking in her surroundings with the most amazing sparkling green eyes. I followed her gaze trying to imagine things the way she was seeing them for the first time. That's when I noticed Alasdair standing across the room carefully studying the goddess-like creature before him. Seeing his obvious admiration caused me to let out a small chuckle, catching everyone's attention.

In a swift move, Citlali who had remained beside Zoe and me until now quickly moved past us and approached the girl.

"Natalie, this is Zoe and Viviana," and motioned us forward.

Zoe extended her hand, "Nice to finally meet you, Natalie, I'm Zoe."

"Thank you, and likewise. I'm Natalie. But of course, you already know this." She blushed. "And you, you are Viviana." She smiled, extending her hand to me, which I accepted in my own.

"Yes, that would be me. You may call me Viv. And welcome." I found myself smiling easily with her.

"Finally, the Linx are complete. And now the fun begins." Mr. Caberletti's voice sang through the room.

"So, we are complete at last, what now?" Ollin queried.

"Like I said, the fun begins. Natalie has already been to the Lummi Reservation. We flew her in through Vancouver BC, it was much easier that way." He laid her weapon on the island countertop. The expression on her face told Ollin, Zoe, and I exactly what thoughts and feelings were running through her mind at that moment. We'd all confided in each other about how our weapons made us feel. The sense of power and ownership made for a quite indescribable feeling.

Natalie grasped the handle of her boomerang weapon and caressed it with her other hand. Her element gave itself away in her eyes, which sparkled a most alluring green. I felt a soft rumbling beneath my feet. Ollin and Zoe looked at each other with questioning glances and then at me.

I reached out a hand once more toward Natalie, but Alasdair stopped me.

"Don't do that. Her element is still raw. She knows nothing about controlling it yet. It could be dangerous." He gave me a look that reminded me of the first time we'd touched one another at Elder Thomas's house.

Natalie smiled coyly, "Do you all have your weapons now?" We nodded in the affirmative. "Great! When do we get to test them?" She looked around the room expectantly.

I was impressed with her eagerness. For someone who'd been as left out of the secret all her life as I had, she seemed much more enthralled by the possibilities.

"We just started training with Citlali today. She's training us in the art of warfare." Ollin mused.

"Trust me, you're not very far behind." Zoe offered.

"The four of you will train every day after school and in the mornings when possible. Don't make too many plans for the weekends as those will need to be open to whatever The Calpulli deems necessary." Citlali stated. "I'll get all of you measured for your gear. Once that's done you may rest. You have school tomorrow."

Her eyes filled with fear, Natalie looked anxiously

from person to person. Tears threatened to spill over at any moment. Visibly shaken, she took a few steps back from the island, and from the rest of us. Zoe and Ollin each looked as if they were preparing for the possibility of Natalie releasing her element, as did Alasdair. Citlali seemed un-phased and looking at Mr. Caberletti. I wondered why she wasn't trying to calm Natalie's element as she always did mine.

Mr. Anderson who'd always seemed perfectly content with quietly coexisting, unlike his daughter who was a natural leader, stepped up to Natalie. Immediately, I looked at Zoe to gauge her reaction. But Zoe seemed totally unperturbed. She possessed uncanny control which was something I would have to learn.

"What's the matter?" His voice was cold and sharp. Apparently, Zoe had inherited this from him.

"I don't want to go to school," Natalie responded, barely remembering to breathe.

This had been my same fear and probably Zoe's as well.

"It's not a choice. Besides, the other four will be right by your side." Mr. Anderson stated.

"Four?" She asked, a bit puzzled.

"Yes, Alasdair is also registered."

Natalie looked at Alasdair who gave her a soft smile. It was nice to see he was capable of such a thing, considering he'd been so nasty towards me. But then again, I didn't look anything like Natalie.

Just as quickly as I felt anger rising from within, I

experienced a calming that was no longer a stranger to me. Citlali.

I shot her a dirty look, as Mr. Anderson continued speaking.

"Unlike your previous school, here you'll come home every day. You'll only be there for less than seven hours each day. You won't have to wear a uniform, and I think you'll find the informality of the place quite different from what you've been used to." Mr. Anderson finished off and returned to my father's side.

His comments seemed to put her at ease as she placed her weapon back down on the counter. Citlali took that as her cue.

"OK, the four of you follow me into the study. Humberto, will you please assist me? I'll measure while you write?" She winked in his direction.

"Of course, it will be my pleasure." He said with a smile.

I almost gagged. Were these two flirting?

CHAPTER TWENTY-SIX

Ollin volunteered to be measured first, to which Natalie, Zoe, and I had no objection. As he stood for Citlalli, it was obvious he was flexing every inch of himself, sucking in his gut and puffing out his chest. I simply rolled my eyes and looked away. Ollin being typically Ollin, too quick to show off, or maybe this was just his way of facing his fears? Who knew? But either way, I didn't like it. His cockiness reminded me of Vitale. Was Ollin the Vitale of our Linx? *Good grief, I certainly hope not.*

Just then my phone vibrated. I reached into my pocket assuming it would be another message that would go unanswered. However, it wasn't, it was my cousin Brian.

"I'm coming over for a visit," is all it said.

I fumbled hurriedly attempting to reply. But my phone slipped from my fingers, falling to the ground and shattering its screen. I let out an irritated moan as I retrieved it and evaluated the damage.

"With that brand, you might as well get a new phone. It costs just as much to replace the screen." Natalie said in a mournful voice.

I returned my gaze to my phone, but the lower half of the screen was completely black.

"Zoe, may I please borrow your phone?"

She gave me a quizzical look but pulled hers from her back pocket and handed it over.

I moved away towards the furthest window in the study and sat in the window seat as I dialed Brian.

"Hey! Where exactly is it that you are headed?" I asked quietly as soon as he picked up.

"I'm sorry, who is this?"

"Oh. My bad. It's me, Viv, I'm calling from Zoe's phone. Long story. Anyway, where are you going?" I pressed.

"To see you. I spoke to Uncle Henry, and he asked me to check in on you. He mentioned you will be staying at the ranch for a bit and that you are officially in public school." There was a smile in his voice that I personally didn't find cute.

"Oh gosh, yes. But, I'm wondering why dad called you? Never mind, we can chat when you get here."

As I was about to hang up another voice chimed in, "I'm visiting too," My cousin Eric. My objection went unheard as the other end of the connection went dead. I sat there briefly wondering what on earth had possessed my father to call Brian, and why would he bring Eric along? Zoe approached me.

"Everything alright?" She asked as I handed her back her phone.

"Yes. No. Ugh! My cousins are headed over here, right now," I told her as I looked out into the dusky night. *What if something happens while they're here? What if Natalie has an episode?* After all, I was still attempting to get my own element under control.

"Oh!" She replied as her already pale skin went even whiter. "But why? Why are they coming?"

"I don't know, Zoe. I'll be right back, I'm going to speak to my father."

I ignored everything else that was going on in the study as I rushed out towards the guest house. I didn't bother knocking as I barged right in finding my father, Mr. Anderson and Mr. Caberletti seated at the table. Gustav was peeking over my father's shoulder, and Jim stood leaning against the wall with a coffee cup in his hands. My sudden arrival caught them off guard, and they looked up at me in surprise.

"Dad, may I please have a word?" I demanded as I walked assertively towards the French doors leading out to the deck.

I heard the door close behind me.

"What's going on Viviana? Have you forgotten your manners and how to knock?" He didn't sound too pleased, but I really didn't care.

"Why did you call Brian? Do you know he and Eric are headed this way right now?"

"Is that what this is all about? You're upset because your cousins are coming to visit you?" He challenged.

How dare he? How dare he take that tone after everything I'd been going through, and the secrets he'd kept from me?

"That's just great! You're mad at me for being upset? Have you thought about how any of this might implicate them? Or is that something only I and the others need to worry about?" I huffed, not backing down. "You seem to think that a simple apology was sufficient for keeping the Linx secret from me, instead of preparing me all this time. I'm seventeen Dad! Did you forget that? I get it, you've been trying to protect me. But has it crossed your mind that you might have been doing more harm than good?" I looked away as the tears flooded my eyes.

The evening was still. Not a single sound could be heard as another moment of silence ensued.

"Brian knows. He's known since Mom fell ill." He moved around the deck.

I stood there in shock. *Brian knew? He knows?* Unsure of whether I should be mad or not, I took in a deep breath.

"You know dad, I'm not surprised anymore. It seems you thought of everything. All except for me, right?" I said it sarcastically, but I was more upset than anything. "I'm headed back to the house. Brian and Eric should be here soon." I turned without giving him an opportunity to stop me, opting for the long way back, circling around to the front of the main house.

As I reached the pond out front, I noticed Brian's car in the driveway. The house was lit brightly now, and I could hear Eric and Ollin commanding the conversations. Soccer, of course, was the topic. I wasn't ready to rejoin the others, so I found my way to a cement bench, tucked under a weeping willow, overlooking the motionless pond. In the background, the trickling sounds from a separate water feature provided a calming effect. I pulled my knees up to my chest and closed my eyes. A simple moment of uninterrupted tranquility, where the past several days wouldn't consume my thoughts, I pressed my face into my shoulder so my shirt could absorb my tears.

The soft, consistent trickling of water evoked a calm within me, as my tears subsided. A few moments to escape reality and think of absolutely nothing allowed me to compose myself. Finally, I wiped away the tears, regained my composure and made my way back into the house.

I found Brian staring out the back anticipating my return. Zoe was sitting alone, carefully observing my cousin. Alasdair was in the kitchen, but Natalie, Citlalli, and my uncle must still have been in the study, which reminded me, I needed to be measured.

"Hi," I said quietly, but still loud enough for Alasdair, Zoe, and Brian to take notice and look up. Ollin and Eric were engaged in animated conversation.

Quickly, Brian moved in my direction, carefully

studying my face. He was probably wondering if my father had already admitted to me that he knew.

"Hey." He smiled as he hugged me. "How are you?" He asked, then quickly added, "So, public school?" smiling good-humoredly.

"Yep. Public school. It's terrible." I said, playing along.

I noticed both Alasdair and Zoe carefully watching us, but I wasn't ready to include them.

"I need to take care of something. Care to join me?"

He nodded and followed me into the study, where I introduced him to Natalie and Citlalli.

Natalie went quite red in the face when he shook her hand, but she quickly recovered. After some brief small talk, she quickly dismissed herself leaving Brian and me with Humberto and Citlalli.

I opened and closed my mouth, unsure if I should say anything about Brian knowing, but it appeared that area had already been taken care of.

"We know that Brian knows, Viviana," Humberto admitted.

I let out a sigh of relief, thankful that I wouldn't be outing my father.

"Come over here so I may measure you and we can talk." Citlalli calmly requested, her voice was like a soothing melody.

"So, do all of the Calpulli know that Brian knows? And you're all OK with it?" I queried.

Citlalli recited my measurements to my uncle as he replied to my question.

"Yes, we know, and actually it was Mr. Caberletti's idea. He knew we needed someone close enough to you to help us, someone you trusted. We didn't know when you'd come into your element, so we wanted to ensure that we were on high alert."

Of course, I thought to myself. *More secrets and they'd even recruited one of the only people I would ever confide in.*

Brian must have sensed my irritation as he moved closer to my side.

"I wanted to tell you, but I was sworn to secrecy. At the end of the day, I knew the truth would eventually reveal itself, and we'd have the opportunity to talk." He reached for my hand. "I almost told you when you came over the other day, but I knew Zoe and Ollin had no idea, so I had to wait."

So, they didn't keep it only from me? Not that that made me feel better, but at least I wasn't left in the dark on my own, once again.

CHAPTER TWENTY-SEVEN

When Citlalli and Humberto had finished up the measuring, they gave Brian and I a moment of privacy, for which I was thankful. Although I'd been upset at being kept in the dark, I was equally pleased that Brian knew. My cousin was my best friend, and it was nice to have someone I could turn to that wasn't involved in the chaos that was becoming my life.

"So, what do you think of all this? The prophecy? My powers?" I asked him.

"I'll admit, it was a lot to absorb when I first learned of it. I even thought Uncle Henry had gone crazy. But when he demonstrated his powers to me, I had no choice but to believe him. Either that or I was just as crazy," he chuckled.

I pondered his words. *My father demonstrated his powers to him.* It occurred to me that I had yet to see this from him or any of the other Calpulli.

"It was impressive, he generated and manipulated in his hand something I couldn't understand. When he took me to the others, and they too revealed their powers I knew it was all true. I knew I had to help you."

"It's a lot, isn't it? I mean, I feel like I'm way in over my head. How am I or any of the Linx supposed to save humanity? We're only seventeen years old. Two of us are just learning about all this, and all four of us have yet to come into our powers fully. Apparently, this is supposed to happen when we're all together, which we now are." I paused as I thought about it. *What is the linking of the Linx supposed to look like? And when?* "I've still had zero training with my element, and the same with Natalie. I have no idea what to expect."

"It will be interesting to see how they handle your element." He said.

"What is that supposed to mean?" I pressed.

"Your element. The Calpulli have very little experience with fire elementals, right? Just the writings as far as I understand."

I remembered a previous reference to this, but I hadn't given it much thought.

"Right. I haven't even considered that."

"Well, I know I can't offer much, but I'm here for you. And now that you know that I know, nothing has changed, right?" He touched my shoulder to offer reassurance. I nodded affirmatively.

"So, how do you like school?" He smiled mischievously. "Did you know, we are now official rivals." He said winking.

"We are?"

"Yep! But hey, it's all good." Brian joked.

"Well, I'm not sure how much allegiance I'll have to this school or how much time I'll even have to get to know anyone. It's pretty safe to say any banter will likely take place between you and Ollin. He seems to fit right in."

"I'm not surprised. Over at Tahoma High, we even caught wind of the new students. A few of the guys on my team are wondering if Ollin and Alasdair will be joining the school team. Boy's season is in the spring. I might even encourage them to try out." He laughed as I jokingly poked him in the shoulder.

"Don't even! We have a lot to focus on, they can't afford any more distractions than they already have." I cut my comment short as I realized it probably sounded more like an insult than anything else. "Come on, let's go join the others."

Natalie and Zoe were deep in conversation. Ollin and Eric had already joined Alasdair in the kitchen raiding the refrigerator and pantry. Alasdair looked up from his phone as we joined them. He studied me carefully as if something about me had changed. I brushed it off as just my imagination.

"You ready to go, Eric?" Brian asked.

I cautiously looked towards Zoe, wondering if I'd read too much into a possible crush she might have on my cousin.

"Already Dude? I was just going to have a snack," Eric responded.

"You can have a snack at home. Let's go. I have a paper I need to finish for tomorrow." Brian walked away not even giving Eric a chance to argue. "See you all later." He said over his shoulder.

I could have sworn he'd looked straight at Natalie. Zoe probably thought the same as she followed his stare back to her. I had to admit, it was hard to keep your eyes off of her. And from her body language, she seemed to know it.

As soon as they left, Zoe was on the verge of going too, but then Citlalli and Humberto found their way back into the common space we were sharing.

"Good, you're all still here. Did your cousins leave?" Humberto inquired. I simply nodded in response. "Great! Well, that gives Citlalli and I some time with you all. Change into some comfortable clothes and meet us in the arena. Bring your weapons."

I just showered! Wasn't the earlier training enough? But I gave in without a word and retrieved the weapons bag from the study. Heaving it over my shoulder with a grunt I started towards the arena as the others were heading off to change.

Loud snorting and neighing erupted from the stables as I approached. The horses were restless in their stalls as I walked through. A sudden crash reverberated from one of the stalls causing me to whirl in that direction. One of the stallions was pawing the ground, and snorting loudly. Head lowered, the horse's long mane fell forward over its face but not quite enough to hide the fear in the deep black eyes. The sight sent a chill through me.

I took a few steps back not daring to turn my back on the stallion. The horse took a few steps closer.

What in God's name is happening? I thought as the stallion's muscles and tendons began growing larger. The animal was transforming right in front of me, taking on more of a beast like form.

I gasped when a hand suddenly covered my mouth from behind.

CHAPTER TWENTY-EIGHT

A voice whispered in my ear, "Don't make any sudden moves. I'll guide you backward. If it charges, break to your right and climb that ladder into the rafters." I nodded slowly, letting Alasdair know I'd heard and understood as I allowed him to maneuver me slowly backward.

The super horse looked like a perfectly formed piece of artwork, designed to intimidate. Except it was real, and it was right there in front of me, with foam flying from its muzzle.

We were retreating successfully until I tripped on something and stumbled. That slight error was enough to set the beast in motion, and Alasdair gave me a mighty shove toward the right as he broke to the left. I tumbled to the ground, rolling in the dirt and hay, looking over my shoulder to locate the snorting beast. Alasdair had diverted its attention giving me enough time to regain my footing and make it to the ladder. As I started scrambling upward, I looked back once more to see that Alasdair had his sword drawn. His weapon seemed magnified, charged by his element, as it released a thunderous bolt of electricity. The beast stood up on its hind legs, front legs flailing in the air. It let out the most horrifying sound I'd ever heard a horse make, like all the demons in hell had been released.

Suddenly the animal shifted its attention back towards me and charged in my direction, dirt flying from its hooves, creating such a cloud of dust that Alasdair was temporarily obscured from view.

Frantically I resumed climbing the ladder, but too late. The horse rose on its hind legs attacking the ladder directly below me with its front hooves. I held on for dear life and shrieked with fear as the bolts anchoring the bottom of the ladder tore loose from the cement mooring. Now each time the horse struck the ladder, it danced against the stable wall.

The sounds of its striking hooves and the fearsome neighing set off the other animals, soon drowning out all other sounds.

I was terrified as I felt myself losing my grip, but then miraculously I regained my footing on one of the rungs and threw my arms around the side rails to avoid being flung off.

I looked down to see Alasdair shouting at me over the noise, but I couldn't make out his words. Suddenly the horse wheeled around on Alasdair. In a blind rage, the beast charged him. "Run Alasdair, run," I screamed. He desperately tried to outmaneuver the animal but to no avail. The horse seemed to anticipate his every move.

Alasdair threw lightning bolts back over his shoulder at the beast, one after another, but it was barely enough to slow it down. I had immediately resumed climbing the ladder into the rafters when I heard a loud scream and the thunder of hooves on the ground as the super horse charged at full gallop. I looked to find Alasdair now running after the horse, once more attempting to divert its attention from the rest of the Linx who seemed frozen in place with Natalie screaming at the top of her lungs.

"Run," I yelled. But they didn't move. "Run." Still nothing.

My element erupted as fear, anger, and my survival instincts combined to energize me. I conjured a flame and aimed it in the direction of the horse, but it missed, lighting fire to a pile of straw on the ground. Again, and again, I hurled balls of blue flame trying to keep pace with Alasdair's lightning bolts.

Zoe seemed to snap out of it first as she pulled on Natalie and Ollin. Ollin looked around to find where Alasdair and I were, by following the directions our elements were coming from.

"Run!" I yelled yet again. Ollin quickly shook off

his confusion and grabbed Natalie.

Zoe made every attempt to hold off the beast by hurling shards of sharp ice at the animal, but it seemed nothing we did could stop it. I worked my way through the rafters until I was directly above them. The others kept circling, in an attempt to avoid being cornered.

I found safe footing among the rafters and did my best to clear my mind as I called forth my element, creating a huge ball of blue flame. The radiant light slowly built between my hands as I held them wide apart, palms facing each other.

"Throw it now! Now!" I recognized Alasdair's voice, and I released it with all my might.

I stood there in complete astonishment as Alasdair discharged a bolt of his electric energy directly into my fireball. Together our two elements struck the beast and halted its mad rush. The energy of our combined elements sent the beast staggering backward, releasing a massive plume of smoke as it landed on the ground.

We all watched not sure what to expect as the horse returned to its original size. Whatever had possessed it seemed to have departed. That's when we heard the clapping from the stable end of the arena.

Approaching us slowly out of the darkness were the Calpulli. It had all been a test devised by them.

CHAPTER TWENTY-NINE

"What on earth is wrong with you people, are you trying to kill us?" Natalie cried, as I rejoined the others on the ground.

"This was but a simple test. The Moon God and his followers will show no mercy nor will they give you any warning." Mr. Caberletti stated sternly. "That was nothing compared to what the four of you will be facing soon. By the way, Alasdair, that was excellent thinking on your part to combine elements. What made you think of it?"

My eyes sought out Citlali who stood quietly among the others.

"I'm not sure, sir. I guess it was intuition." Alasdair said convincingly.

"Well, it was wise of you to follow your intuition. As for you Natalie, and Ollin, I know this was only your first time, but I'm disappointed that neither of you reacted with your element. Zoe, I am glad you finally did." Mr. Caberletti finished.

The words still didn't go over well with Zoe, who seemed genuinely concerned.

"You are correct, Mr. Caberletti. This just goes to show how truly unprepared we are. We need nonstop training," Zoe said, her actual thoughts seemingly elsewhere.

"Very well then, let's all form a circle, it's time," Citlali said. From her tone, I decided she didn't necessarily mean it was time to train. This was something else.

CHAPTER THIRTY

The dimly lit arena held the lingering scent of ozone from the recent skirmish. Thinking about that skirmish caused me to recall seeing Mr. Anderson hauling the weapons bag out of the way before it got trampled. Citlali now retrieved the bag from him, laying it out on the ground and untying the leather straps. One by one she held our weapons out to us as we stepped forward to retrieve them.

"Now form a circle," she directed as we moved to comply. "Alasdair, please stay here by my side."

He quietly took his place next to her.

"The rest of you, please move back. No matter what happens, you must not intervene. Hold your positions," Citlali cautioned.

Ollin stood between Natalie and me with an irritating smile. *No shame in that boy* is all I could think.

"All right. Hold your weapons up in front of you with both hands. Make sure you keep your feet apart to help maintain your balance. You are going to need a solid stance." Citlali smiled. "No matter what happens, do NOT close your eyes. I need you to focus on everything that's happening."

Zoe and I glanced at each other and then at Natalie who looked petrified.

"Now, focus your minds on your body's core as this is where your element resides. Feel for it in there and slowly begin to create a strand of energy, pulling it out of you, through your body, your arms and right out into your weapon. As your energy reaches your weapon, aim it toward the center of the circle and release it gradually until it connects with the energy of the others." Citlali took a slow, shallow breath. "Whatever you do, maintain your positions, especially you Natalie since this is all new to you."

I found my element immediately as did Ollin and Zoe. I knew they'd already strung their elements as their weapons were pulsing with energy. Carefully I pulled my element through watching my spear tip begin to glow slightly and pulse as my element simply waited for my command.

Citlali coached Natalie as we waited.

"I don't know what I'm doing. I've never called it out on purpose, it's always just come on its own," Natalie whined.

"Your element cannot manifest on its own, Natalie. Your fear brought it out in the past, but now you must learn to conjure it by your command. Instead of waiting for something to happen, you need to feel the power of your element from within," Citlali calmly explained.

"Think about the times your element has manifested. Remember that feeling deep in your core and focus on that feeling. Don't say anything, just focus." She paused, "Now, move that feeling slowly up to your chest. Don't close your eyes, keep them focused on your weapon," Citlali continued. "Feel your element move through your arms then to your fingertips and finally out into your weapon and hold it there. Just focus it right there."

I dared to peek just then and caught the anticipation in Natalie's face. I knew she was experiencing for the first time what it was like to feel like she had some control. After all, just a few days earlier I had been in that same position.

"Take that feeling of your element and think of it traveling in a very thin line through your weapon as it begins to radiate out from the tip." Citlali slowly stepped away from Natalie as the ground started to rumble, "It's OK, Natalie. Just keep thinking of the strand of energy."

Citlali had moved somewhere behind me as she gave the following instructions.

"Okay Linx, allow your elements to connect in the center. Be careful though as they might give you a jolt," she added.

All of us carefully watched our elements reach the center and approach Natalie's which was already there. Ollin's was first in a glistening grayish color, Zoe's in an icy blue, and mine in a flickering reddish orange. Our elements began to intertwine with the emerald green of Natalie's element, causing a gust of cold wind to swirl around us. Immediately my element wanted to fight it off, but I held firm as Citlali had instructed. It was Natalie who threatened to break our concentration as the ground rumbled more around her.

"Natalie, control." Zoe shot at her.

"I'm trying!" Natalie countered, a look of desperation on her face.

"Just focus on the center." I offered.

The feeling was inexplicable as our elements continued to vie for control over the others.

I carefully observed the faces of the other Linx. Natalie's still full of fear, while Ollin and Zoe seemed to be embroiled in a stare down contest as their elements fought for prevalence. I found something about the scene amusing.

It had become a tug of war between air and water, Ollin and Zoe, and neither seemed to realize it, as Natalie slowly regained control over the rumbling beneath our feet.

Ollin and Zoe now seemed even more eager to outdo one another. Their elements no longer mere strands but fully formed tornado and water sphere. They seemed doggedly determined to wipe out each other's element.

Finally, I'd had enough of the tit for tat and decided this exercise needed to get back on track. With intense concentration, I willed my fire strand to encroach upon the inner circle. With a flick of my spear, I sent my element's string in a swirling motion that engulfed the other three strands and slowly tightened around them until it had compressed them into one tight, unified mass. The action caught them all off guard and caused Natalie to falter slightly, but she quickly regained her composure. A crackling sound spread throughout the circle, as each of the strands began to glow and pulse in unison, and the mass at the center tightened into a basketball size globe which shone like a miniature golden sun.

The wind gradually subsided, and the fear in my companion's eyes slowly turned to awe.

Something more than a mere demonstration of elements had just happened. Despite ourselves, we felt a new bond had been created between the four of us as we stood there with our weapons pointed toward the center. If Citlali hadn't spoken and reminded us there were others present, we might have stayed that way much longer.

"You may lower your weapons now. Go wash up and get some rest. I'll meet you here tomorrow after school for weapons training," she instructed.

None of us spoke as we walked away from the Calpulli. There was now an energy between us that we found invigorating. I allowed myself the luxury of a smile when we reached the backyard.

"That was crazy," Natalie whispered. "What was that?"

"The connection," Zoe said, matter-of-factly.

"I guess we're now officially The Elemental Linx," Ollin suggested.

Yes, it would seem this had been the awaited connection that would unite the four of us. What next? Perfect our skills? Master our elements and our weapons? Then what?

I locked the door behind me when I reached my room, once again making my way to the shower.

I showered quickly then put on pajamas and slipped into bed, wondering how exactly we'd manage school and training. There I was once again, worrying about having to put on a show of normalcy for the public? Surely there had to be a good reason?

Though my eyelids were heavy, I kept telling myself I needed to remain awake to think through a plan. However, at that moment something else forced its way into my thoughts. I could hear celestial voices and recognized them instantly as the Seraphim.

Bright, white light illuminated my entire room, so bright I couldn't see beyond it. Threes winged beings stood before me, softly smiling as they spoke to me. They spoke in unison and their voices blended as one.

"It is time Viviana. You must find the Five Pendants of Creation before the Moon God, and his followers do. Without them, The Tetrad Prophecy cannot be fully realized." Their wings fluttered continually, sending small ripples through the air. "Four of the pendants are scattered about the earth, and the fifth pendant's location will be revealed to you when the time is right. Go now. Do not hesitate or you will surely run out of time."

Their image began to fade.

"Wait! How do I find them? The earth is so large," I said panic stricken.

"You must go to the land of the Mayari myth, and there within the caverns of the place named during the Spanish conquest you will find the first pendant." The voice faded along with the apparition.

I jumped out of bed and retrieved a pen and paper from my backpack and wrote it all down while it was fresh on my mind. *What the heck is the Mayari myth? Caverns? Which Spanish conquest for heaven sake? Do they have to speak in riddles?*

I then rushed to the closet to pull on some clothes, stumbling as I shoved my legs into my skinny jeans. Slipping on a pair of tall boots, I rushed to Zoe's room, quietly tapping on the door. I waited and tapped again. When she didn't respond, I opened her door only to find her room was empty. I looked in the bathroom and the closet, nothing. Then I went toward the master bedroom where I heard voices. I waited for a minute by the door trying to make out the voices but I couldn't, so I knocked.

"Hi!" Natalie said as she pulled me into the room.

I froze at the door, realizing I hadn't been in the room since my mom was still among the living. I quickly shook it off when I noticed both Ollin and Alasdair were there.

I wasn't sure why, but a pang of jealousy hit me then. *Were they having a consultation without me*? I suddenly felt embarrassed, maybe I wasn't wanted. Insecurity certainly had a way jerking my emotions around.

"I'm sorry. I... um. Never mind, it's not important." I lied, spinning around and rushing down the stairs. I was glad I knew exactly where Jim kept the car keys as I quietly made my way through the house to the garage. I looked out the garage window to see which car was parked in the driveway and grabbed the keys from the hook, bursting out the side door.

As I put the car in reverse Alasdair rushed out the front door waving for me to stop, but I didn't care. I opted not to turn on the lights until I was out of the driveway.

On a sudden impulse, I reached into my cross-body bag, fished out my mini tablet, and called Brian via an app, who luckily was still awake.

"Hey. Sorry to bother you so late, I'm just leaving the ranch, and I need to talk. Can you meet me somewhere?" I asked.

"Okay, Viv. Well, there's a 24-hour diner not far from you, Sheri's. Do you know it?"

"Not really. Is it new?"

"Bring it up on your navigation system, and I'll meet you there. If you get there first, grab a table and order us some coffee. I suspect this will be a long night," he mused, and I was glad of his understanding. I was also glad I had someone outside of this overbearing circle that I could turn to and trust when I felt the need.

I had pulled over to the side of the road so I could find the diner on my phone when Alasdair's car pulled up beside me. I glanced over at him with his rolled down window but ignored him as I continued punching in the location on the navigation. I soon found out it would do me no good though as he pulled his car across in front of me, blocking me in.

He walked over and tapped on my window.

"What do you want?" I asked, only lowering my window halfway.

"Where are you going? And why did you leave?" He sounded concerned.

"Look, I don't have time for this. I need some space right now, away from all of you and everything," I said, rather irritated.

"Is that what you call it? You got mad because we were gathered with Natalie. Did it ever occur to you that she has no one? And she is just now learning about all of this?" Now he sounded annoyed.

"Well then what are you doing here? Go! Go and be there for her along with everyone else. I really don't care. What bothers me is that none of you even thought to include me. We're supposed to be a team, and at the first opportunity you all ditch me."

"You didn't give anyone an opportunity! I was right behind you when we came out of the arena, but you didn't even notice as you quickly distanced yourself from everyone and disappeared into your room. Zoe was the one that got Natalie settled into the master bedroom because she didn't even know where she was supposed to stay."

He had a point. I didn't even think about that. I had rushed to get away. I hated that he was right, again.

"OK, fine, I'm a bad hostess. Are you done? I need to be somewhere."

"Where do you possibly need to be at this hour? Come on Viviana, don't do this. Please. The four of you really need to be bonding more than anything, not creating separation," he said quietly.

I thought about Elisha, Vitale, and Tadeo. I wondered what they were all like during their first few days. Vitale had said that Tadeo would have been the leader if he weren't so reserved, but it was Isaiah, or should I say, Alasdair, that took on the role because he was more willing. Vitale had also said that Tadeo was the last to come into his element after his own mother died, kind of like me. I pondered that for a moment, suddenly feeling terrible knowing that he knew I'd lost my mom as well, and how he'd seemed to be protecting me and in return, I challenged him every chance I got.

I shook my head, willing the thought away and returning back to the task at hand.

"Look. Like you said, Natalie needs support. I get it. Trust me, I do. I suppose I overreacted thinking you all really didn't want me there. I don't know. I don't know anything anymore, I'm an emotional mess, and

I need to get away from the house and the others for a while."

"Then you'll allow me to accompany you. Because you can't be out here alone. Especially not you."

I thought back to the night he'd returned from his outburst. A shiver ran through my body at the memory of the screeching. The hair on the back of my neck all stood up.

"Fine. I guess it wouldn't be good if you simply let me go on my own. And the last thing I want is for anyone to get into hot water over my actions."

He looked at me as if my words caused him pain.

"What?" I said.

"Surely you know?"

As we stood there holding each other's gaze, I felt my element coming to life. My chest rose and fell a little more rapidly as I held my element at bay. Without warning, Alasdair reached out and carefully tucked a loose strand of my hair behind my ear. His fingers were gentle and only caused my insides to further ignite. Thankful for the night sky that hid the sudden onset of a blush, I quickly looked away trying to not make a big deal of his tiny show of affection.

"Yes, I know. You care about this mission as much as I do." I attempted to sound as aloof as possible as I looked away from him. But then he leaned in my window and gently drew my face back toward him, sending every mixed signal possible through my mind.

"Yes, of course, the mission," was all he said as he released me.

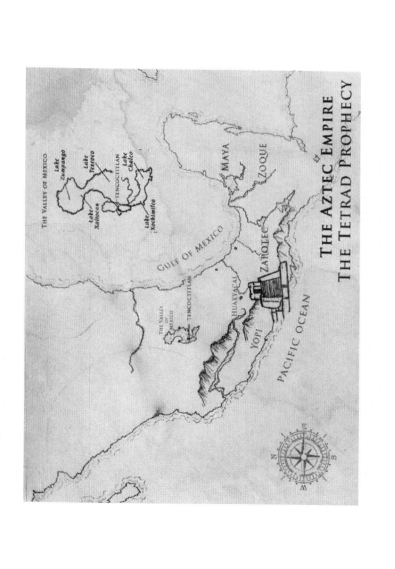

THE VALLEY OF MEXICO

*Lake
Zumpango*

*Lake
Texcoco*

TENOCHTITLAN

*Lake
Chalco*

*Lake
Xaltocan*

*Lake
Xochimilco*

GULF OF MEXICO

TENOCHTITLAN

THE VALLEY
OF
MEXICO

HUAYACAL

MAYA

ZOQUE

ZAHOLEE

YOPI

PACIFIC OCEAN

THE AZTEC EMPIRE
THE TETRAD PROPHECY

Thank you, readers! I've enjoyed researching and writing this book, and look forward to sharing the rest of the series with you.

There is an abundance of Aztec myth and legends, but I've always enjoyed The Creation Story. The story is widely known among Aztec historians and aficionados, like me. So I knew as I set off on this journey, that I had to share this important piece of Aztec history.

I'd like to thank the many keepers who guard Mesoamerican history so beautifully, treating this with the utmost of care. I had massive amounts of literature at my disposal via the various forms of written words.

My favorite site, although not all inclusive, Aztec-History.com, does a fantastic job of capturing who the Aztec's were in everyday life. And providing factual information, in an easy to research format.

Although I grew up learning about Aztec history, I still find myself often tongue tied with the Nahuatl dialect. Not even my proficient fluency in the Spanish language can save me from this, which is why it was important for me to provide the Lexicon at the beginning of the book. I hope you find this useful.

Finally, I can't wait for you to read book two, Five Pendants of Creation, as we follow the Elemental Linx on a scavenger hunt like mission around the world, and they find themselves further riddled with other myths and legends wherever their journeys take them.

Available Now
A Shining Star
A compelling story of
Faith…Life…Love…Redemption…and Spirit.

Coming Soon
The Tetrad Prophecy Series
Book Two: Five Pendants of Creation
Book Three: Pillar of Life & Four Blood Moons

Contemporary Inspirational Romance
Anika's Way

Acknowledgments

First and foremost, to my editor, William H. Gould, thank you for believing in me from the very start. The journey here has been worth it.

I'll never find enough words to thank my eldest son who's sat with me through countless hours of research. So often his eyes are what I need when my vision fails me. Literally.

Thank you to my fellow authors and friends, Elyse Bruce & Thomas Taylor. You two have provided more than writing advice, you've provided a friendship since the inception of this venture; you've gently nudged me back on the correct path, helping me refocus on my love for the craft.

Author Angelique S. Anderson, thanks for allowing me to be me; writer and friend extraordinaire!

Kait Reed, you, my friend, inspire me on every level.

To the never a dull moment in the Facebook community, Writers' Group. I joined, left, and came back. You all are a hoot!

And my friends in the Multiple Sclerosis | Fibromyalgia | Chronic Pain Support Group. Remember, every day is a new day, and the fact that you are reading this is your loving reminder. As always, gentle hugs to you all.

To the many talented fellow writers who have inspired and helped me along the way.

To you, the reader, for taking a chance on me.

Last but not least, to my parents Maria & Enrique, my one, and only brother Jose, my dearest friends who've cheered me on like no other, Dyana, Jennie, Michelle, and Tara aka T-rad.

Thank you, each and every one of you.
All Glory To God!

Follow Me

Website: rosesarehappy.com

FB: facebook.com/itsrosecastro

Instagram: @itsrosecastro

Twitter: twitter.com/RoseCastro